The
Golden Dream
of Carlo Chuchio

Books by Lloyd Alexander

The
Golden Dream
of Carlo Chuchio

Lloyd Alexander

SCHOLASTIC INC.
New York Toronto London Auckland Sydney
Mexico City New Delhi Hong Kong Buenos Aires

ISBN-13: 978-0-545-11017-4
ISBN-10: 0-545-11017-3

12 11 10 9 8 7 6 5 4 3 2 1   8 9 10 11 12 13/0

Printed in the U.S.A.   40

First Scholastic printing, September 2008

Book design and illustration by Laurent Linn

For young dreamers, and old ones

The
Golden Dream
of Carlo Chuchio

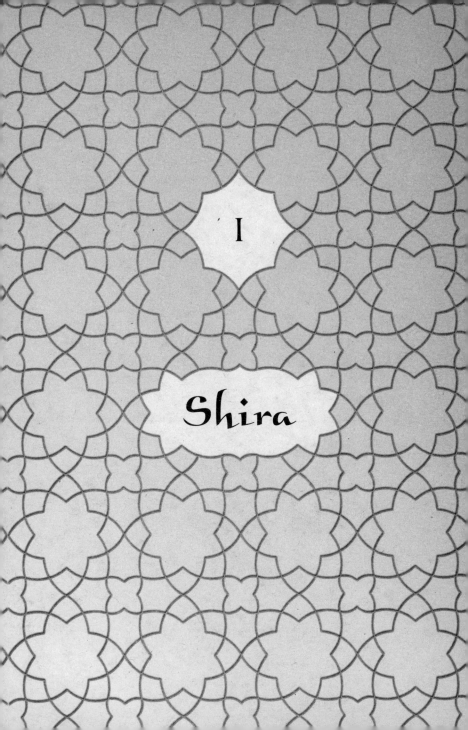

I

Shira

When the world starts falling about your ears and intensely disagreeable things are happening to you, it's always a comfort to blame somebody else. But—who? In my case, not Uncle Evariste. No, he did the sensible thing. Certainly not my fellow clerks and scriveners. None of it was their fault. I'm casting around trying to think of someone other than myself.

Ah. I have it. Of course. The bookseller. If he ever existed in the first place. But I know he did. Should I curse him? Or thank him for all that came later?

To begin, then, on a sparkling blue afternoon in our port city of Magenta. I had taken a stack of receipts and shipping records for deposit with Casa Galliardi, the merchant bankers. It was no more than a few hundred yards from my uncle's office and warehouse, but such errands took a long time. Instead of promptly going back, I would loiter at the docks.

Moored at the wharves or anchored in the harbor, there must have been anything and everything that could float: cargo vessels; often a galleon big as a house; long, slender craft with three-cornered sails; a flock of little fishing boats. Our Isle of Serrano was a horn of plenty, overflowing with fruits and vegetables to feed mainland Campania. But our real cash crop came from Eastern ports. Silk. Jade. Carpets. Cinnamon, cloves, nutmeg—I could smell them in the air. Uncle Evariste imported and resold these precious goods. He did well. Except for me.

When he had nothing more urgent to do, he would yell. Usually on Mondays, Wednesdays, and Fridays. He was a methodical man.

"Carlo, Carlo, what's to become of you?" he would burst out. Then, once he got into the spirit of the occasion, he would pull his beard with one hand and fling the other heavenward.

"Why? What have I done to be plagued with a thankless daydreamer? Eh? Eh? I'm asking. You tell me."

"Truly, Uncle," I said, though his question was not specifically directed to me, "I don't know."

I was, in fact, more or less grateful to him. He and my father had been partners until, years ago, a vicious fever took away my parents along with many of our islanders. Uncle Evariste gave me board and lodging; and, such as it was, my occupation in life.

"Oh, I've seen you—don't think I haven't," he ranted on. "Sitting with your nose in some book of rubbish. Like an idiot. Carlo Chuchio—Carlo the jackass. The dimwit. Carlo the chooch."

Here, he used the vulgar street pronunciation of "chuchio." He thrust his beard at me. "Do you know? That's what they call you behind your back."

"Sometimes to my face," I said.

"Keep on like that," he said. "You'll amount to—to what? Nothing!"

Then he would go off muttering to himself. And that was mainly all we had to say to each other.

Now, the bookseller. Yes, that day. On my long way back from Casa Galliardi, I left the quayside, the sailors bawling in every language, and wandered through the market square. My mouth watered at the mounds of blood oranges, lemons, figs, olives. The best on the island. (We sold the second best to Campania.)

Next to the melon vendor stood an open-air bookstall with an array of old engravings pinned to a length of clothesline. Shelves leaned every which way, with shabby volumes crammed one against the other. Surprisingly, I had never before noticed it. Naturally, I had to stop.

Rubbing his hands, the bookseller stepped over to me. A little man with a stringy beard, a narrow, beaky face. A total stranger.

"My good messire," he began. "And what does the worthy gentleman fancy?"

He spoke with an unfamiliar accent. I said nothing. For one thing, I was taken aback—but hardly displeased—at being called a worthy gentleman. For another, I had no idea what I fancied.

"A tractatus on mathematics? Military engineering? No? Geometry? Architecture? No, again?" He gestured at the sagging shelves. "Perhaps the art of writing love letters, with examples to be copied. Useful phrases for every circumstance, to woo your lady fair."

He drew closer, cocking his head, studying me like a tailor calculating my measurements for a suit of clothes.

"No, messire, I see none that fits."

I was about to turn away when his eyes lit up. He snapped his fingers.

"Of course. Exactly."

Without looking, he reached behind him and pulled a small, thick volume from a shelf. The leather cover was scuffed, the stitching had come loose. The pages were mottled and dog-eared, nearly falling out of the binding. He fondled it with obvious affection.

"A curious collection of old tales. I promise you will find it most enjoyable."

He pressed the book into my hands. Truth to tell, I wasn't all that much interested. After a few moments, though, I was spellbound. I couldn't take my eyes away. Leafing through, I saw these were tales of amazing voyages, carpets that flew in the air, caves of glittering treasures. If, at first, I had no idea what I fancied, I knew now. This.

The bookseller must have sensed my excitement. He beamed and bobbed his head. "A gentleman of fine taste and judgment. A rare volume, messire. And what a joy to match the perfect book with the perfect reader. These days, alas, it seldom happens.

"For you," he went on, "I make a special price. Less than I paid. But, after all, what is profit?" He sighed. "And yet—and yet I hate to part with it."

"You won't have to," I told him.

He blinked at me. "Eh? Why so?"

I answered simply and sadly that I had no money.

His smile collapsed. "There's the trouble with these young gallants," he muttered. "Empty pockets. It's a contagious disease."

I would have given back the volume, but he raised his hands.

"Ah—no. You like it too well. I haven't the heart—aie, my generous nature will be the ruin of me. So, so—Keep it, then. Yours. Free."

I had to protest—a little. Purely as a formality. My refusal was neither strong nor convincing. Especially since I did not loosen my grip on this prize and had no sincere intention of doing so. When he disregarded my feeble show of reluctance, I deluged him—several times over—with wholehearted thanks for his kindness.

"That remains to be seen," he said. "Go away. Before I come to my senses and change my mind."

Never had I made the journey back to the office at such breathtaking speed. Not that I was eager to do my work. I could not wait to examine my gift more closely.

The copying clerks, Simone and Melchiorre, dutifully scribbling away, barely glanced at me. I climbed onto my stool, pushed aside the bills of lading, the manifests and inventories, and plunged into the book. It was even more thrilling than I'd supposed.

To the shock and astonishment of my colleagues, I stayed perched at my desk until sundown. They left me still poring over the tales.

At dinnertime, with my prize tucked safely inside my jacket, I pleaded vaporish ailments, a headache, an upset stomach, and begged to be excused from the evening meal. Uncle Evariste, mumbling something like "What a chooch," was glad enough to grant my request.

I bounded up to my quarters in the low-ceilinged attic, lit the candle on the table beside my cot, and flung myself onto the straw mattress. In case I had missed so much as a word here and there, I began reading again from the first page.

Later, Silvana, our housekeeper, worried I might be fatally ill or starving to death, carried in a tray of leftovers. Seeing me alive but preoccupied, she warned me to stop whatever I was up to or I would do myself a mischief, and went back downstairs.

I had never suffered from lack of appetite; nor been so caught up by tales of gigantic birds, genies popping out of lamps to grant every wish. How to choose between eating and reading? I resolved that knotty question by doing both at the same time.

The pages, however, kept falling loose. They soon parted company with the cracked leather binding. The spine had split down the middle. It was then I noticed something had been stuffed into it.

It was a rolled piece of parchment covered with crisscrossing lines and squiggles. A diagram? A map of some sort? But I saw no directions, no bearings. Curious, I laid aside the book to study it.

I realized I had been looking at the back of the sheet. When I turned the parchment over and smoothed it out, I saw indications of mountain ranges, rivers, towns.

At first, I judged it too vague to have any use or meaning. But, no, as far as it went, it was fairly precise. There was an inset drawn at one corner, an enlargement of a portion of the area. My heart began racing.

It showed, in some detail, what appeared to be a city of considerable size—or what had once been a city. The sketch depicted only the ruins of a wall circling the jagged stump of a tower, perhaps a fortress, and the rubble of a central square. What set my heart pounding was a notation in a spidery, almost unreadable hand: "Royal Treasury." That was enough to make my thoughts gallop as fast as my pulse. I had, by now, convinced myself this was a map of hidden riches. If my book was a treasure, I had found yet another treasure inside it.

But there was a difficulty.

Whoever drew the map had known the region very well; so well, indeed, he had not troubled to name the location. What city? What mountain range? What lake? What river? They could have been anywhere in the world.

My candle guttered out. I lit another. I tried to stay calm and make sense of what I was dealing with. My eyes fell on a single word squeezed onto the edge of the parchment.

That word was "Marakand."

Then everything fell into place. I understood exactly what I was seeing. I had handled enough shipping papers to know Marakand, across the sea from Magenta, was the great trading center in the Land of Keshavar and the gateway to the Far East. I was holding nothing less than a map of the main route to the fabled realm of Cathai. Called the "Road of Golden Dreams," it had made the fortune of so many merchants who'd traveled it. Everything Uncle Evariste imported came one way or another by way of this Road of Golden Dreams.

Despite my spinning head, I had begun shaping a plan. I put aside all trivial questions. What if the map's original owner had gone back and dug up this vast wealth? No, I had his map; and, for all I knew, he was likely dead. What if someone else had accidentally stumbled upon it? I denied that possibility. What was in the royal treasury? Gold? Diamonds? How to carry it home? How long would it take? Mere details.

My plan was simple and straightforward. When I showed my uncle what I'd found, he would eagerly launch an expedition. Since the map belonged to me, naturally I would be the leader. And claim the lion's share. There would be more than enough to go around.

We would be rich beyond imagination. And I? Carlo Chuchio? Carlo the Donkey? No. Carlo Milione. Carlo the Millionaire.

I began laughing and hugging myself. Then I stopped short. In the midst of this golden dream, a thought wormed its way into my head. I tried to pay it no mind, but it grew bigger by the moment. I had discovered something that shattered every hope. In the blink of an eye, it threatened to snatch away my fortune even before I had it in my hands.

2

What I discovered was: my conscience. I never had much occasion to use my conscience. I never suspected I actually owned one. Evidently, I did. I did not like it. It was making my head hurt and my stomach turn queasy.

It kept jabbing at me. A question about the map. Conscience insisted it did not belong to me. I disagreed. We had a not-very-friendly conversation.

Myself: "You're talking nonsense. The bookseller gave it to me. Free. A gift. He said so."

Conscience: "Wrong. He gave you the book. He didn't give you the map."

"He did, too," I protested. "He gave me the book. The map was in the book. It comes to the same thing."

"Does it?" Conscience said slyly. "Answer me this: Did he realize it was there?"

I mentally shrugged. "How should I know? Maybe not."

"Maybe not?" said Conscience. "Probably not?"

"All right, then: Probably not."

"Say, rather: Most certainly not. He gave you the book out of kindness and generosity. He had no intention of giving you the map. It was a mistake, an accident."

"So?"

"Let me put it this way," said Conscience. "Suppose you gave your old coat to a freezing beggar. And suppose you'd forgotten some gold pieces in the pocket. You'd want them back, wouldn't you?"

"Of course."

"Now we're getting somewhere. Very good. So. What are you going to do?"

"Keep the map," I said.

"You're disgusting," said Conscience. "You haven't understood a word—"

"What do you want from me?" I said. "I'm a chooch."

"Even a chooch can do the right thing. Sometimes, at least. Tell me, have you ever had a piece of grit in your eye? And you rub and rub, but you can't get it out? And only make it worse? I promise you'll have a piece of grit that won't go away. It's going to sting and smart every day for the rest of your life."

"Get out," I said. "Let me be."

I fell back on my cot and slept. Badly. Next morning, I went to the market square with the map in my pocket.

The fruit and vegetable dealers had just set up their stands. I walked—not quickly—past the old woman and her display of melons. I had my hand on the map, ready to give it to the bookseller.

I saw no sign of him.

It must have been too early. I asked the melon vendor what time her neighbor would arrive. She recognized me, she had seen me on my errands; and, in Magenta, everyone knows everyone else's business.

"Bookseller?" She gave me an odd look. "What bookseller?"

The one, I said, with a stall next to her own.

"Nobody like that." She kept shaking her head as I insisted I had been there only yesterday. Had he moved somewhere else? Where could I find him?

"What are you blabbering about?" she said. "No bookseller. I'm here thirty years. I should know if there's a bookseller. No such person. Not yesterday. Not now. Never."

I was running short of patience. "I bought something from him—that is, he gave me something. Right there. That very spot."

"Don't waste my time." She went back to arranging the melons. "What a fool," she said under her breath. "Poor uncle, such a burden for him. But, nothing to be done about it. There's a chooch in every family."

What she had told me puzzled and, at first, troubled me. I thought it over and finally understood. There was a simple explanation: The bookseller had opened his stall within the past day or two. She hadn't noticed. His trade had been too slow; he changed to a better location. I walked all around the marketplace, up and down the side streets. Not a trace. No question, he was gone. He could have left Magenta altogether.

Satisfied I had done my duty—my conscience was keeping its mouth shut—I hurried to the office, eager to put my plans in motion.

No sooner did I set foot inside than Melchiorre stepped up. My uncle, he announced, demanded my presence immediately. He was grinning so happily I expected to be yelled at, though it was only Thursday. I was unworried. As soon as he learned what I had in mind, my offense, whatever it was, would be forgotten.

I found Uncle Evariste hunched over the table in his counting room. Beside him, black-robed, looking like a melancholy crow, stood Messire Bagatìn, his accountant.

Since Uncle Evariste didn't pull his beard or yell, I suspected this might be serious.

"You," he said, in a voice icy enough to give me gooseflesh, "you've ruined me."

Before I could ask what he meant, he pressed on:

"You've made mistakes before. I put up with them for the

sake of your parents. But not this time. With your daydreaming and woolgathering—do you know what you've done? Of course not.

"I'll tell you," he said between his teeth. "You mixed up the accounts. Idiot. You got them backward.

"You wrote down the money I made as if it were money I owed. Yesterday, when you took the receipts to Casa Galliardi, you listed my assets as liabilities. Do you have the least glimmer of the mess you made? Bagatìn can straighten it out—but who knows how long it will take? As far as the bankers are concerned, my account stands at zero. My assets will be frozen. I'll have to borrow money. At ruinous interest. Meantime, I have nothing."

That was all? I gave a sigh of relief. Only a temporary disaster.

"Uncle," I said, "never mind that. I'll make a fortune for us. A thousand times over."

I brought out the map and handed it to him.

He squinted at it for a moment. In a pinched voice, he said: "Where did you get it?"

"From a bookseller," I began. "What happened, you see—"

"Happened? Happened? Who cares?" Uncle Evariste flung at me. "Where is this fellow?"

"In the marketplace," I said. "That is, he was. I went back and looked all over for him. I couldn't find him again. He's gone somewhere else."

"Naturally."

Now the yelling began.

"Make a fortune?" Uncle Evariste cried. "With this? If I had a ducat for every one of these I've seen in my time, I'd be a rich man. A fraud! A ridiculous fake! Trash like this is floating everywhere. For sale to gullible jackasses. How much did you pay?"

"Well, nothing—"

"Exactly what it's worth."

He crumpled the parchment and threw it at my head. And missed. I scooped it up from the floor.

"This can't keep on." My uncle's face glowed crimson all the way to the end of his nose—an effect I had never before produced on him.

"Enough is enough," he said, struggling for breath. "You're no longer in my employ."

This set me back on my heels. Not that I was sorry to be free of my tedious work, but I was also confused. I murmured something about my lodging. I supposed I would still be living in the house.

"No. You will not." My uncle snapped off the words. He was calmer now, which upset me more than his yelling.

"You are a walking catastrophe," he said. "An embarrassment on two legs. I want you to be gone. Away from here. Out of Magenta. Out of Serrano."

I said I didn't understand.

"I don't want you anywhere near me. After what you've done—to have you here? A thorn in my side? You'd make me a laughingstock. My trade would suffer. Who'd want to deal with me? It would cost me more to keep you than to let you go."

My uncle was not a cruel person, neither wicked nor heartless. He was simply a man of business. I saw his point. In his place, I probably would have done the same.

"Even so," he went on, "family is family." He motioned to Messire Bagatìn, who took a leather purse from the folds of his robe and passed it over to me.

"The best I can do with what cash I have on hand," Uncle Evariste said. "It should be enough to tide you over until you get on your feet. Oh, very well, you can have your dinner and stay the night here."

I thought I saw a passing shadow of sadness on his face. In any case, he wasn't gloating.

"Tomorrow," he said, "you'll go to Campania." Back to his everyday gruffness, he added:

"With so many fools there, one more won't be noticed."

Again, thanks to Silvana, I had dinner on a tray in my attic. Also, at my request, she kindly gave me a needle, thread, and a pair of scissors. I had a night's work ahead of me. Not in the way of packing: My few extra garments fit easily into a canvas shoulder bag; along, of course, with my book of tales.

The purse—Uncle Evariste had been more generous than I expected. I found a good number of gold pieces as well as a quantity of lesser coins.

The small change I left in the purse, ready to hand. The gold pieces—I had the clever idea of stitching them into the hem of my cloak and traveling clothes. It took longer than I thought, since I kept stabbing myself each time I plied the needle.

Finished at last, I had to admire my work. I was, so to speak, wearing my fortune on my back. I would not be the most fashionably dressed; but, no doubt, the most expensively.

As for the map: I smoothed out the wrinkles and sat staring at it a long time. Uncle Evariste judged it worthless; he, if anyone, recognized worthless when he saw it. If a fraud and forgery, I might as well tear it into confetti and toss it out the window.

So I would have done. I stopped short each time I began. Yet against my uncle's opinion, against all reason and logic, I believed it was real. Knew in my heart it was real. Anyway, there was no harm in taking it with me. I slid it into the lining of my jacket, slung my bag and cloak over my shoulder, and went downstairs.

The rest of the household lay sound asleep. I did see a light from under the door of the counting room. My uncle and Messire Bagatin had no doubt been toiling the night away to clear up the mess I'd made.

I had no stomach for leavetaking. I stepped quietly into the street.

The cobblestones were slick and wet. It was well before daybreak. Too early for the fruit and vegetable sellers, the marketplace stood empty. I headed for the docks. I felt glad enough to be free of the office, counting room, Casa Galliardi, the whole business. Not, however, as glad as I expected to be. It was, it occurred to me, the first time in my life I had been without a home.

I cheered up considerably as I neared the quay. This could, I told myself, be all for the best. In fact, I already had a plan.

If, as my uncle claimed, there were so many fools in Campania, surely I could find one to hire me. For something. This time, I resolved to do well. If I was diligent, seriously buckled down and paid attention to my work, my career—whatever my career might be—was bound to prosper. Uncle Evariste would have nodded approval at my common sense. He had, unwittingly, done me a favor by throwing me into the street. I thanked him for it.

As soon as I gained sufficient wealth—it shouldn't take long—I would lead my own expedition eastward and prove the map real.

There was no doubt in my mind, I would discover the treasure. Then I would sail triumphantly home, gloriously rich, to the awe and admiration of Uncle Evariste, Messire Bagatìn, Silvana, Melchiorre, Simone, every citizen of Magenta, every inhabitant of Serrano, Campania, and far beyond. Carlo Milione.

At the moment, I needed cheap transportation north to the mainland. I walked along the docks, hoping to find a fishing boat or small coasting vessel.

I saw one likely craft and hailed a burly man who had the air of being the captain.

"Where away?" I called.

"Bound east," he called back. "Bound east for Sidya."

I knew that name. Most of my uncle's goods came through this port, the busiest in Keshavar. If Marakand was the gateway to the Road of Golden Dreams, Sidya was the doorstep.

"Want passage?" The captain held up a lantern. "You look like a strong lad. Listen, I'm shorthanded. Help with the bailing, a few light duties, and I'll take you there free. How's that suit you? We have a bargain?" He added, "I want to catch the tide, so be quick about it. Come aboard."

I did.

3

The captain's offer of passage to Sidya in exchange for my work turned out to be no great bargain for either of us. I spent most of the voyage being seasick. I rendered up what seemed to be every morsel of food I had eaten during my entire lifetime. At least, I provided good-natured merriment for the crew. They assured me they had never seen a living human being turn such a bright shade of green.

Our little cockleshell of a boat leaked so much I was amazed it floated. I helped as best I could with the endless bailing. When the wind died and the sail hung limp as a dishrag, I lent a hand at the oars. Sometimes we made no headway at all. I doubted I would ever set foot on dry land.

Seeing me in despair, the captain promised landfall the next day. I had noticed he never consulted his compass or any other navigating device. How, I asked, could he be sure? He pointed upward.

"The sun. The stars. Better than any of your fancy compasses. Above all, this." He tapped his nose. "Every port has its own stench. Set me blindfolded in a rowboat, I'd make my way straight to Sidya. No mistake. I smell it already."

He was right. After a time, I, too, sniffed an odor in the wind. Not, as I expected, the heady aroma of precious spices. More like garbage. And we did, in fact, reach Sidya Harbor late the next afternoon. As we tied up at the dock, I made ready to climb the stone steps from the landing stage to the quay. The captain held me a moment by the elbow.

"Tell me, lad," he said confidentially. "Ever thought of following the mariner's trade?"

I answered that I hadn't really considered it.

"Take an old sea dog's advice," he said. "Don't."

Even so, we parted company on good terms. Despite the wreckage of my digestive equipment, and not remembering when last I had a night's sleep, once on solid ground I felt in fine fettle and eager spirits. However, the din along the quayside split my ears and rattled my brains. I was hardly able to collect my wits, let alone decide what next to do.

If Magenta was a bustling port, Sidya bustled a dozen times louder and faster. Never had I seen so many comings and goings, embarkings and debarkings, sailors, dock hands, merchants in turbans and long robes or garbed in the fashion of my own part of the world. And all shouting at the top of their voices—not in their mother tongues but in trade-lingo.

Cobbled together from just about every language, trade-lingo was common coin where goods and money changed hands. Not only in all ports, but from Marakand, throughout the Land of Keshavar, the Road of Golden Dreams, and beyond the borders of Cathai.

Idling around Magenta harbor, I had picked up a good bit of it. (In time, I came to patter the lingo as well as anyone; and spoke it as if by second nature.)

At the moment, however, I was not concerned with trade-lingo but with saving my neck. Barely had I taken two paces when a mighty army of street urchins besieged me. They wore hardly enough rags among them to put together one suit of clothes. I first thought they meant to murder and rob me then and there in broad daylight. They had higher ambitions.

Pulling and pushing me in all directions, they implored me—for the sake of my comfort, well-being, and the health of my immortal soul—to follow them to one inn or another. I later learned they scraped out a living by hustling travelers to these lodging houses; for which service they received a coin or two as commission.

The choice was not mine to make, the decision taken out of my hands when yet another ragamuffin appeared. Taller than the rest, nearly my own height, this new arrival scattered the army like so many ninepins and shooed them away when they tried to regroup.

"Do not listen to them," warned the newcomer. "They are shameless liars and riffraff." Every bit as ragged and grimy as the others, the youngster sported a head cloth that looked as if it had wrapped countless generations of previous heads. "Bless your good fortune I came in time to save you from being cheated. I shall be taking you to the finest lodgings in Sidya."

Quick as a conjuring trick, this individual relieved me of my shoulder bag. My cloak would have joined it if I hadn't wrestled it away.

Since my bag had already been kidnapped, and seeing not much difference among the urchins, I thought I could do no worse than to follow this one.

"My name is Khargush. 'Rabbit,' as you would call it," my self-appointed benefactor went on. "And you, mirza, will be grateful and thank me generously."

Rabbit, I noticed, used the respectful address "mirza," all the while towing me disrespectfully along one of the streets leading from the dockside. I appreciated the courtesy.

"The Joyful Garden of Happy Travelers," Rabbit continued. "There is no inn like it. You shall have the biggest room in the house and live like a king."

My guide—or abductor—chattered on about the luxuries in store for me: the sumptuous meals, the delights of the hammam, which I understood to be some kind of sweat bath or steam chamber.

If this Joyful Garden of Happy Travelers turned out half as good as he claimed, my journey would have begun well. And Rabbit, under the various layers of grime, seemed a likable sort.

At last, running out of attractions to praise, my conductor added:

"Wherever else your journey takes you, mirza, you will not forget your days there. Your home away from home. Indeed, many of you ferenghis lodge with us."

The word *ferenghi*, I knew, applied to any Westerner. Not an especially complimentary term, it was common usage. I took no offense. Still, I bridled a little, hearing it applied to myself. I could not help replying, in a bantering tone:

"Well, now, Messire Rabbit, I'm glad to have made your acquaintance and I thank you for all your heartfelt concern. I ask, only out of passing curiosity, what makes you so sure I'm a ferenghi?"

Rabbit grinned. "Mirza, you smell like one."

I let that pass. We had come into the courtyard of a rambling structure of timber and mud brick. A balcony ran the length of the upper story. I glimpsed sheds, outbuildings, and, judging by the aroma, stables.

Rabbit ushered me inside. If someone had put the port of Sidya under one roof, the effect, as far as noise and confusion were concerned, would have been the same. Rabbit motioned toward a large alcove. There, the landlord bent over a wooden counter barricaded with piles of account books and cash boxes.

I first thought to ask his professional opinion and advice on how best to make my way to Marakand. I decided to put that off for a quieter moment when I could hope for his closer attention. My turbaned, heavily-bearded host was overoccupied in dealing with arriving and departing guests. He barely had time to accept my payment for several days in advance, flick the beads of an abacus to calculate the exchange rate of my Magentan currency, subtract his commission, scribble an unreadable receipt, and note the transaction in one of his ledgers—all of which he did with lightning speed—and wave me away.

Rabbit led me up a rickety flight of stairs to a long, open-sided gallery. At the far end, a door hung ajar, relaxed on one hinge. I ransomed my bag with a couple of the coins I had received in change—probably too much, for I had no idea what they were worth.

Rabbit showered me with blessings, more salaams and gestures of gratitude than the situation required—which made me suspect I had, in fact, vastly overpaid—and then vanished, leaving me to fend for myself.

My sea voyage, though relatively short, had exhausted me. My muscles began aching all at once, the aftereffects of rowing and bailing. My stomach, thoroughly emptied, growled and grumbled. I could hardly keep my eyes open.

I squeezed my way through the sagging door and stepped gladly into my room.

4

First, I thought I had been mistakenly led to the steam bath. Stifling, drowning in a sea of hot air, I began dripping with sweat. But Rabbit had told me the truth. Windowless, lit by the glow of oil lamps on low tables here and there, this surely had to be the biggest room in the house. What Rabbit had neglected to mention: There was space enough for several dozen occupants.

Most seemed to be present, in various stages of packing or unpacking. Straw pallets lay in ranks along the walls. A few of my unexpected roommates snored peacefully on them. The rest gave me a nod or wave of the hand and paid no more attention.

Some wore Western garments. Others, though clearly ferenghis, had adopted the local costume of long caftans and loose pantaloons. All carried a dagger or wickedly curved knife in their waistband.

My book of tales had led me to expect palaces. If not carpets flying through the air, there should be at least one or two on the floor. Rabbit had promised I would live like a king among kings. If that was so, my fellow kings were a hard-eyed, hard-jawed collection of monarchs.

Sleeping accommodations appeared to be on the basis of first come, first served. I found a pallet at the far end of the room. No royal body was stretched out there. I claimed it as my own and sat down, my bag between my knees.

Now followed a difference of opinion between stomach and head. Stomach screamed to be filled with something, anything. Head pleaded to be laid horizontally on the pallet.

Stomach, in the end, outshouted head. I picked up my bag, slung my cloak over my shoulder—I had no intention of leaving either item alone and undefended—and went downstairs.

The odor of cooking drew me to the common eating room. I had heard that diners in this part of the world sprawled at ease on piles of soft cushions. Here, no doubt to entice the ferenghi trade with a more familiar setting, were long trestle tables and benches. A cavelike fireplace belched hot, aromatic clouds while slabs of unidentifiable meat roasted on spits. Tall metal urns bubbled and hissed. I squeezed onto the end of a bench. My server eventually arrived: None other than Rabbit carrying a brass tray, having changed the profession of abducting travelers for that of feeding them. We recognized each other. I decided against commenting on my quarters in favor of attacking the meal Rabbit set in front of me.

Whatever the platter held, I neither knew nor cared. No sooner had I started to engage it than a long-shanked, long-necked fellow detached himself from the crowd milling around the eating room. He sidled over to me. He had a way of glancing furtively in one direction while moving in another.

About a handsbreadth of space remained on the edge of my bench. My uninvited table companion put one haunch on this area. The other haunch strove to join it. He elbowed me to yield a little more room—he was not only a sidler but a nudger—until he gained most of a seat.

If I was wearing my fortune on my back, this nudging sidler looked as if he had dressed in every garment he had ever owned. He wore layer upon layer of threadbare shirts, vests, short jackets, and long coats. A scrub of beard started at no definable point and scrawled over his lean face with no particular destination. A round cap of heavy cloth perched on his head. It reminded me of one of our big Serrano mushrooms that somebody had trod on.

He pointed a hawk's nose at me and drew closer, pressing a hand to his heart—wherever it lay beneath all his clothing.

"With your permission and kind indulgence, mirza," he began, "my name is Baksheesh."

I offered my own name. I would have replied that he needed neither my permission nor indulgence to call himself whatever he pleased, but he hurried on:

"I beg a thousand pardons. What, only a paltry thousand? More than there are stars in the sky. Forgive me for daring to intrude on Your Most Excellent and Worshipful Self, muddying the clear waters of the Oasis of Your Contemplations, disturbing the Majestic Progress of Your Fragrant Digestive Process.

"How could I help it?" he added. "To see one of such noble bearing, Your Eye of Command flashing as if the sun shone from the Precious Ivory of Your Brow? I was drawn by the Lodestone of Your Presence. You are a ferenghi—"

"I know I am," I said. "Now you're going to tell me I smell like one."

"That, too," said Baksheesh. "But no, I only wish to learn what brings Your Magnificence to a place like this."

I wasn't such a fool that I couldn't recognize blather when it was poured all over me. On the other hand, it was better than being called a chooch.

So I answered, only in general terms, that I was traveling on private business to Marakand and perhaps a little distance beyond.

"Alone?" My table companion's eyebrows went up. "Then Your Graciousness shall require a camel-puller."

I shook my head. "I don't have a camel."

"But you will. You must. A necessity in those parts. Allow me the joy of providing my humble services. It will be the greatest honor, the crowning glory of my existence."

I admitted I had no idea what a camel-puller did and why I needed one.

"As I would be your servant," explained Baksheesh, "so, likewise, is the camel your servant, and I am the servant of the camel. For loading, unloading, guiding the difficult and temperamental creature, being spat upon—sparing Your Immaculate Person that indignity."

During this, I had grown aware that Baksheesh, with deft thumb and long forefinger, was all the while delicately extracting morsels from my platter. A sidler, nudger, and a picker into the bargain. Nevertheless, I realized I knew nothing whatever of the mysteries of the camel-pulling profession. I thought it over for a time and nodded agreement.

"O Compassionate One!" cried Baksheesh. "You have my sacred vow, my solemn oath. I swear on the head of my venerable father—whoever he is. I am, from this moment, your faithful servant in all hardships and adversities, shielding and defending you even unto death. Yours or mine. Also, I work cheap."

Rabbit, standing nearby, brought glasses of mint tea. Baksheesh lifted a finger:

"If you could procure a few of those delicious honeyed pastries, the kind with chopped almonds on top. Charge them to the account of my master and dearest friend—what was the name again? al-Chooch?—plus a little gratuity for yourself. Less my commission."

He turned back to me. "Leave all in my hands, Prince of Perfection. The sooner on our way, the better. You shall be eager to go about your business, may it profit a thousandfold."

"Less your commission?" I said.

"Naturally. As for myself," Baksheesh went on, "I would prefer to be unnoticed in Sidya, and I can best be unnoticed if I am not here at all. As the saying goes, the law ends where the walls of Marakand begin. Beyond them, you could slit a fellow's throat a dozen times over. Who's to care? . . . And so, Navel of the Universe, I bless the very shadow you cast. I kiss your footprints in the sand. You have saved my wretched life at the risk of your own."

This, I thought, was going a little too far by way of gratitude.

"Baksheesh," I said, "all I did was give you a job. I hardly call that risking my life."

"As we are companions, I must be honest with you," Baksheesh said behind his hand. "You may find this hard to believe, Most Exalted Among All Ferenghis, but I have enemies. The latest one—a wart on the nose of humanity! A festering boil! A running sore!

"You must understand, Fountain of Benevolence, the laws of Keshavar are severe. For the least offense, the harshest punishment is exacted. Ears and nose cut off. And other bodily appendages.

"That's before the trial begins," he added. "Found guilty—and one is always found guilty—it gets seriously worse."

Baksheesh was squirming around—a squirmer on top of everything else—in such discomfort I suspected he had a direct, personal concern. I asked him straight out if he was in trouble with the law.

"A mere technicality." He shrugged. "But, yes, that worm, that scorpion had the impudence to complain to the magistrate that I stole a clove of his garlic."

I was relieved to hear that. No law in the world would go to such length over so small a matter. Baksheesh, I realized, had a tendency to exaggerate. I almost laughed in spite of his heartfelt indignation. Still, to satisfy my curiosity, I frankly asked if he had, in fact, stolen the garlic.

"No, no," he protested. "That is to say: Not exactly. It was, you see, along with a handful of other spices, stuffed inside a roasted chicken. Unfortunately, the chicken was accidentally reposing on a silver platter. And the platter, by strange coincidence, happened to rest on a silver tray. I had no heart to break up such a tasteful arrangement. To keep them together, what could I do but take them all?

"Before I was able to perform that service, the house-holder thoughtlessly came into the room. That mean-spirited descendant of baboons actually tried to lay hands on me.

I might have been injured! I ran like a gazelle. What if I had sprained an ankle?

"Those are insignificant details." Baksheesh waved them away. "The point is, Noble Benefactor, our lives and fates are bound together. As you are my master, the law judges you an accomplice and holds you equally responsible. The same punishments apply. Alas, we could both end up like kebabs on a stick.

"Never fear," he added. "Under the Sheltering Wing of Your Innocent Countenance, we shall sneak boldly from Sidya. Once in Marakand, we complete our profitable business and remain there in ease and luxury until the case is forgotten. As it will surely be."

"Baksheesh," I said, "thank you for confiding in me. Since you have been so honest and forthcoming, I can be no less. I am going far beyond Marakand. I intend to follow the Road of Golden Dreams."

"What are you saying?" Baksheesh nearly toppled off the bench. He stared horrified at me. "Ah. Now I understand. You frightened me for a moment. Paragon of Sly Wit, you are jesting with me. Ha-hah! I laugh with appreciation of Your Ineffable Humor."

His jaw dropped when I assured him I was serious. "Road of Golden Dreams? Road of Nightmares! Say, instead, the Road to Jehannum, lowest pit of Hell! Deserts of salt, deserts of stone, mountains of fire—"

"You've been there?" I asked.

"Of course not. Thief I may be—on occasion. A fool? Never. Furthermore, there is no such road.

"That is to say, no single Road of Golden Dreams," he went on. "No one straight path. Dozens. Like a spider's web, crossing and crisscrossing. Some trails are usable, some near impossible, all of them bad.

"Once—who knows how long ago?—the Land of Keshavar was a grand empire. Parzya, it was called. But it grew too large and stretched too far. It couldn't defend its borders against so many tribes nibbling away at them. Parzya fell of its own weight. What's left of it? Nothing. Ruins in the sand.

"The tribes have never stopped bickering. The Road? It depends on which warlord's fighting his neighbor for some stretch of it, and squeezing tolls from passing caravans. Try skirting the warlords and their strongholds? Then you have robbers in business for themselves. Roving bandits. Packs of murderers.

"Trust me," Baksheesh urged. "We shall be happy in Marakand. I beg you, Excellence in All Things, venture no farther. I say this for your own good. Take my advice. You'll live to thank me."

I thought this over while Baksheesh calmed down enough to gobble the pastries Rabbit brought. If the roads were as bad as he claimed, I truly would be a chooch to go alone. Finding another camel-puller? The next might be a worse rascal.

"Baksheesh," I said, "you have a choice. Go with me or not, as you please." I told him we could part company here and now with no hard feelings. I pointed out, however, he had given his solemn oath and sworn on his father's head.

"Did I say that?" He chewed his lip. "Perhaps so. I must have forgotten. Bless you for reminding me. I am nothing if not a man of my word. Within reasonable limits."

I suggested something else he might want to take into account. I made slicing motions at my nose and ears. Had he mentioned being turned into kebabs on a stick?

Baksheesh squirmed. "Ah—now that you bring that up. Yes, well, for your sake, O Peak of Perfection. So be it."

That matter settled, one thing puzzled me. If the Road of Golden Dreams was so dreadful, I asked, why would anyone wish to follow it?

"O Radiant Youthfulness"—Baksheesh sighed and shook his head—"the world is a terrible place. You'd be astonished at what some people do for money."

He stowed the couple of surviving pastries somewhere about his person, licked his fingers, and followed me upstairs to my royal chamber.

There was as much racket at night as during the day. My fellow kings were asleep. I had never heard such snoring, coughing, groaning, and gargling all at once in the same place.

I found my chosen pallet still available. I lay down on it

while Baksheesh, luxuriously scratching himself, occupied the floor. To safeguard my map and hidden fortune, I put my bag and cloak under my head and slept in my clothes.

That is to say, I didn't sleep. I tossed and turned on the straw. Baksheesh's warnings spun in my brain. Assuming only half of what he said was true—which half? I forced myself to close my eyelids. They sprang open again.

Baksheesh crept in beside me, whining that hard surfaces made his elbows ache. I was too tired to push him out. He nudged and squirmed until I clung to the edge of the pallet. He did not snore. He was a wheezer.

I pulled my cloak over my head. With no way of sorting fact from falsity, I decided it was all wild nonsense, overblown travelers' tales.

That eased my mind. I finally slept, as deeply and solidly as I had ever done. I woke refreshed, strengthened, in the best of spirits.

Until I realized one thing. I was naked except for my underdrawers. My cloak, bag, every other stitch of clothing—gone.

So was Baksheesh.

5

I sprang to my feet. The room was empty, the other travelers had gone about their business. I ran to the gallery. The sun was high; I must have heavily overslept. I tried to keep my wits, but I was jumping back and forth over the edge of panic. My trove of money, my present belongings, my future hopes had all vanished in the blink of an eye, and Baksheesh along with them. I threw modesty to the winds and raced three steps at a time down the stairs.

In his alcove, the innkeeper sat massaging a string of beads. The Keshavaris, I gathered, employed this device to calm themselves. And very effective it was. When I babbled what had happened, he seemed in no way upset; and, indeed, appeared used to this as all in a day's work.

I noticed Rabbit leaning against the kitchen door, looking on with amusement, finding the sight of myself and my underdrawers highly entertaining.

"You claim your camel-puller robbed you?" said the innkeeper, ignoring my state of undress. He pondered a moment. "Mirza, let us assume you are speaking truth," he said. "In which case, you should have been more prudent in choosing a servant. I must conclude, therefore, you have brought this upon yourself.

"However, since you are a young ferenghi," he added, with a measure of forbearance, as if not much better was to be expected, "and a guest under my roof, I shall do all I can to help you. Travelers often leave worn-out garments behind. I have bags filled with castoffs and can provide what little you need. One shirt or another? Easily replaceable, of no great worth."

I did not tell him of the gold coins and treasure map. That struck me as unwise. For an innkeeper, he had made a generous gesture. I thanked him and said no more.

"At the earliest opportunity, one of my people will sort through the rag bags," he said. "I advise you to go back to your room and remain calm."

I had no other choice. I followed his advice. That is, I went to my room. I did not remain calm. I slumped on my pallet, head in my hands, my thoughts racing to no purpose. The law would be no help. On the contrary. Given that I was an accomplice in crime, I might at best lose my nose and ears; at worst, be impaled on a stick. Either prospect made my flesh crawl. Yet, how could I track down that treacherous camel-puller on my own?

In seafaring terms, I was dead in the water. I could do nothing until I had some rags on my back. In my present halfway naked and wholly impoverished state, I saw no means of—doing what? Making my way home? I would rather be an earless, noseless kebab. Robbed, ruined, a beggar at my uncle's door? Never.

And so I sat and stewed, trying not to lose my mind along with my fortune. I got up, after a time, and paced aimlessly back and forth, as if any kind of activity would clear my thoughts. It did not. I heard footsteps outside. My spirits rose. One of the innkeeper's servants with some clothing—

Baksheesh calmly stepped in.

As soon as I laid eyes on him, I started yelling louder than Uncle Evariste had ever yelled at me. I addressed him in words and terms I didn't know I knew.

Baksheesh, unruffled, dropped a large and lumpy bundle to the ground. He untied the ropes holding together what might have been a sack of doorknobs for all I could tell.

"O Most Fortunate One, how blessed you are to have a servant like my humble self," he said, as if he had never been absent. "Ah—by the way, a camel will be available."

The camel, I suggested, could pull itself from here to Jehannum. I yelled some more, demanding to know where he had gone and what the devil he had been up to.

"Tending to my master's business." He smiled blandly. "As any faithful servant should do."

"My clothes?" I shouted. "What have you done with them?"

"Behold, O Needlessly Perturbed Prince." Baksheesh spread the contents of the bundle. "Lo, all you require is here."

I stared at the pile. I feared the top of my head would fly off. "Those aren't mine."

"They are now," Baksheesh said. "In the bazaar there is a little shop I occasionally visit. I purchased these for next to nothing. Their owners, alas, are no longer among the living, but their garments are in splendid condition. You can hardly see the bloodstains."

"No, you fool!" It was all I could do to keep from seizing him by the collar of one of his numerous shirts. "My own—"

"Sold to a passing ferenghi," said Baksheesh. "At a good price. Less my commission. No, no, yours were not suitable for rough travel.

"I observed your garments were heavy, Worthy Master. Remarkably, most unusually so. Out of curiosity, I had to examine them. Miracle of miracles! Every seam was filled with gold."

"I know that, you wretch!" I burst out. "Where is it? What have you done with it?"

"A traveler who carries gold carries his own death warrant," said Baksheesh. "It is far too valuable. You would have Your Noble But Unsuspecting Throat cut before you spent a single coin.

"I sought the services of a money-changer," he went on, "and obtained trade-currency acceptable everywhere—at an excellent rate of exchange. Less my commission, of course."

Baksheesh produced an oilskin belt fitted with pockets holding much of my new money, and instructed me to loop it around my waist. The rest was in a purse to hang from my neck. The small change left over, he himself would carry.

"To spare you the added burden," he explained. "I shall see to our incidental expenses."

I told him that was all very well, but there was something else.

"This, Fountainhead of Learning?" He fished out my book from the pile. "These are tales of silliness to amuse the young and innocent. Nevertheless, in Your Infinite Wisdom, I assume you have some reason for keeping it."

"So I do," I said. "And one thing more."

"Oh—ah, yes, yes, there is." Baksheesh smacked himself on the forehead. "It slipped my mind. I quite forgot about it."

He extracted my map from one of his coats and handed it over to me. I slid it into my money belt. Baksheesh gave me a wounded look.

"Alas, does this betoken some lack of confidence in your honest, upright servant? Your Worthiness saw fit to withhold your true purpose. Treasure is what you seek. I am more than eager to help you find it. With my assistance, I am certain we shall discover these riches. And you, O Generous One, will surely insist on offering me a modest share—which I shall reluctantly accept.

"But this must be a deep secret between us." He laid a forefinger on his lips. "Not a word is to be spoken."

"Starting with yourself," I said.

Baksheesh, hand on heart, swore agreement; then, piece by piece, hauled items from the bundle which also held a cook pot, a pan, a large butcher knife, and various other utensils. He helped me into loose-fitting trousers, then high boots of leather soft as butter, the most comfortable I had ever worn. He added a shirt and embroidered vest, and a sash for my waist. He showed me how to tie my head cloth, and stood back to judge the result.

It made me a little squeamish, wearing dead men's garments. I shrugged that away. All in all, I was pleased at the effect.

Finally, he handed me a dagger to put in my sash; then held out a long, gracefully curving sword. A "tulwar," as he named it, much like what we in Magenta called a saber.

I could not resist immediately unsheathing the blade, nicked here and there, spotted with rust. Or blood? I brandished it fiercely. No one, I declared, would mistake me for a ferenghi now.

"I wouldn't go that far. But, close enough," replied Baksheesh, dodging out of the way. "And I advise you: Should you ever find yourself in circumstances where weapons are required, never draw your blade. You would only do yourself a mischief. By that, I mean your opponent would slice you to bits."

Not that I had ever done so, but I assured Baksheesh that I could, if need be, give a good, sharp account of myself.

"If you're so sure, then no need to prove it," he said. "Instead, follow the wisest course: Take to your heels. Run like the wind."

I told him I did not consider myself a coward.

"If you will permit me to observe," Baksheesh said, "O Yet Unripe Persimmon, you are too young to know. With luck, may you live to be an old and happy coward. As the saying goes: Better a live jackass than a dead lion."

At his urging, I sheathed the tulwar. One thing, in all fairness, I felt compelled to do:

"Baksheesh, I beg your pardon," I said. "I first believed you had tricked and robbed me. For that, I'm sorry. Forgive me for thinking ill of you."

"An understandable error. But even your reproaches are as precious jewels. I treasure every one. Now let me reveal that I have done yet another invaluable service.

"For your benefit and well-being," he went on, beckoning me to follow him into the gallery, "I have taken it upon myself to hire an assistant."

I halted in midstride. "You did what? A servant to serve a servant? Ridiculous! An assistant camel-puller? I don't need one and neither do you."

"But, yes!" Baksheesh protested. "It is essential. Nay, vital. A matter of life and death.

"Let the Keen-edged Razor of Your Intelligence envision this," he pressed on. "Suppose—heaven forfend, but imagine it nonetheless—you are dangling from a rope over the edge of a cliff. A sandstorm is blowing, ferocious gales are rising. The toe of your boot is cramped between the rocks. You struggle with all your might, you twist and turn, you cannot break free. As my sworn duty, I climb down to save you."

I remarked that I was grateful for his efforts. "And so?"

"Aha!" Baksheesh triumphantly exclaimed. "O Perceptive One, do you now grasp the situation? Think carefully. Who holds the other end of the rope? My assistant.

"And what if some gigantic fish swallows you? And I must crawl into the creature's gullet and haul you out by the heels. Who, then, hauls out both of us?"

"Your assistant," I said.

"Exactly." He hurried on to conjure up scene after scene involving quicksand, snake pits, and so many other dire straits that I begged him to leave off.

"More than that," he persisted. "While I am busy saving Your Precious Life, who will do the cooking? The washing up? And, on rare occasions, the laundry?"

I told him I understood his point, but he kept piling up still more reasons for the absolute necessity of an assistant camel-puller.

I added, with a touch of sarcasm, that he had surely gone to great pains in singling out this remarkable individual.

"No pains at all," he admitted. "I was approached this morning. Beseeched, entreated—well, yes, persuaded. By the one who served us dinner. Our conversation must have been overheard. Some people are shameless intruders and eaves-droppers."

"What, do you mean Rabbit?" I asked.

"So called," said Baksheesh. "And, best yet, the question of wages. True, I work cheap. But she will gladly work for noth-ing. She asks little more than a crumb of bread, a sip of water."

"Hold on a minute," I put in. "I thought we were talking about Rabbit. You said 'she.'"

"Correct," replied Baksheesh. "There is no Rabbit. No such person. Her true name is Shira.

"And, indeed, O Generous Heart," he added, "she is very much a she."

6

You did not realize?" Baksheesh stopped in his tracks. "How is that possible? I thought you knew. I myself saw immediately she was a maiden. It strikes the eye.

"Her voice, her gait, her bearing. Her beard—of which she has not the slightest trace. Her delicacy of features. And other details perhaps unfamiliar to you."

Taken aback, I answered that when we met she was wearing several layers of grime.

Baksheesh shook his head, wonder-struck. "Tell me, O Fledgling Eagle, have you been much out in the world?"

"Only recently," I said.

"That would account for it. I must reveal these mysteries to you another time."

Baksheesh conducted me down the stairs. Since I had paid some days in advance, he took on the duty of haggling with the innkeeper regarding what I had overpaid, and slipped the difference into one of his pockets.

From the main building of the inn, we crossed the courtyard and headed for the stables. Shira—I was still used to thinking of her as Rabbit—would meet us there. Baksheesh had shouldered the bundle; but no sooner had we gone a few paces than he began groaning pitifully.

"It is nothing," he said when I asked what the trouble was. "In my efforts to gather all you needed, I may have done my back a small injury. Pay no mind. The pain—ah, the pain bites like a tooth! But it is worth the joy of serving you. It will pass. Sooner or later."

Baksheesh limped and moaned in such agony that I took the bundle and carried it myself.

"Blessings on you, O Tower of Strength," he said, recovering instantly. "I shall be entirely fit once we are on our way."

Something, however, puzzled me. If the Road of Golden Dreams was so harsh and perilous, why would a young woman wish to travel it?

"As you know, Excellence, it is not my nature to pry into other people's business. That is her affair, not mine.

"I can only tell you she has been a month or so in Sidya, hoping to find work with a caravan. But the caravan masters will not hire a girl. She desires most urgently to reach her home, far east of Marakand.

"With the pittance she earns, how long would it take to save enough to buy a place on even the smallest caravan? And so it falls out profitably for all of us. Best yet, she assures me she has no interest in the fortune we seek."

"She knows?" I burst out. "Wretch, you told her—"

"No, no, I mentioned it only vaguely in passing," Baksheesh protested, "and that was before you swore me to silence. Henceforth, I am the soul of discretion."

At the stables, I saw a rawboned donkey, his rough coat gray as dishwater, tethered to the railing. The animal's ribs jutted like a pair of washboards. Instead of a saddle, a patch of carpet had been strapped to his back. He swung up his head and turned melancholy eyes upon us.

Baksheesh stepped toward him. "Worthiness, behold your steed."

"That's no camel," I said.

"O Marvel of Perception, it is not," said Baksheesh. "I promised you a camel would be available, and it will be. In Marakand, we must determine what route we should follow, and whether a donkey, horse, or camel is most suitable.

"Until then, he will serve us well," he added. "He comes from an ancient bloodline, a creature of spirit."

Of ancient bloodline, I had no doubt. My substitute camel looked old enough to have been foaled at the dawn of time. His spirit I judged to be that of despondency.

"You are skilled, O Splendid One, in the art of riding? No?" said Baksheesh when I shook my head. "Have no fear. You will take to it as a fish to water."

I put down the bundle—dropped it, rather. Around the corner came the former Rabbit and present assistant camel-puller. I had never seen anyone like her. Not in the way of costume, for she was dressed not much differently from myself. I guessed she had picked through the innkeeper's bag of castoffs.

No, not her garb, but all the rest of her. She wore a head cloth loosely tied around hair dark and touched with glints of deep red like our Serrano plums; so dark it shone purple when the light struck it a certain way, like our eggplants. Her complexion was the sun-washed gold of our vineyards' sweetest grapes. I was sorry to fall back on fruit and vegetable comparisons, but I had no better resources. Her eyes, I could only call them almond-shaped, and blue-green as the sea in Magenta Harbor.

I admit she surprised me, and more than that. I meant to offer a graceful, well-turned compliment. I cursed myself for a chooch at what actually stumbled from my mouth.

"Signorina—Dushizéh Shira," I said, "you look very clean this morning."

"And you, mirza," she said, pleasantly enough, "you look better with your clothes on."

Baksheesh insisted it was only fitting and proper for me—

as caravan master, so to speak, to have the honor of riding our donkey. I swung aboard, not as gracefully as I would have liked, with Shira observing my efforts. The two of them loaded on as much of our baggage as the donkey could bear, and shouldered the remainder themselves, including a sack of provender Shira had acquired to feed all of us until we reached Marakand.

And so we headed northward from the inn yard and past the town limits, which greatly relieved Baksheesh—and me, as he assured me we were no longer in danger of being skewered like a pair of kebabs. With Baksheesh leading the donkey by a rope halter, Shira walked alongside. My place of honor was to be squeezed fore and aft between the bundles. I kept lurching from one side to the other. As for honor, I would have called it more the case of a chooch trying to sit on a chooch.

We were an hour or so out of Sidya when we slowed to a snail's pace. Baksheesh, gasping in anguish, began lamenting the condition of his knees.

"An old rheumatism that comes upon me from time to time," he moaned. "I beg you, O Compassionate One, let us halt for the day. Unspeakable misery—my enemies should have this affliction!—perhaps it will ease by morning."

This, I was reluctant to do. It seemed to me we were stopping when we had scarcely begun. Baksheesh gave out such piercing cries that the donkey laid back his ears to escape hearing them.

I saw only one good solution. I climbed off and urged Baksheesh to take my place.

More than willing, he showered me with blessings. All undeserved. My muscles ached from unaccustomed jolting. I was glad to give him my seat in exchange for carrying his baggage. And, yes, it gave me a chance to walk with Shira.

My good deed proved to be a miraculous remedy. Baksheesh dropped off to sleep instantly, chin on his breast, wheezing as much as the donkey.

And so, free of his eavesdropping, I tramped along beside Shira. With no idea what next to do. Leading the donkey, hardly glancing at me, she stayed silent, caught up in her own thoughts. I had an irresistible urge to take her hand. I resisted it.

Nevertheless, after a time, I ventured to make conversation of some sort. I said I was glad to be of help, since Baksheesh had told me she wished to travel in our same direction.

I added that Baksheesh was an eager gossip; and, I gathered, he also told her I had in mind to seek out a fortune.

"As do you all, mirza," she said.

My reason, I began to explain, was different from that of the usual travelers.

"Does it matter?" she said. "One reason is as good as

another. They come to the same, in the end. The Road of Golden Dreams?—Do you know, mirza, who travels it?"

"Merchants, of course," I said. "Who other?"

Shira nodded. "Merchants, yes. For the most part. Serious men. Honest, more or less. Their business is business. The silks, the spices. For their profit and the pleasure of you ferenghis.

"But there are other goods to be traded, and others to do it. Those not on the best terms with the law. With a price on their head in their own countries. Men with no past, or too much past. Those with something to forget, or things they choose not to remember. Adventurers for the sake of adventure. Criminals. Landgoing pirates."

"You seem to know them well, dushizéh," I said.

"Some, very well," she answered. "Some, all too well." She turned those marvelous sea-tinted eyes on me. "And you, mirza? Which are you?"

I said I didn't think I was any of them.

"Or you have yet to find out."

I laughed and answered that I was hardly a criminal or a pirate.

She smiled a little. "Why else are you here?"

And so I told her. If I had accused Baksheesh of being a gossip, I was a worse one. Without making myself look too big a chooch, I explained about the book, the map, Uncle

Evariste, the work I hated—I realized I was prattling on and on. I couldn't help it. And didn't want to.

"At heart," she said, after I ran out of breath and stopped babbling, "you wish to go home. With your treasure, if you find it. But your home, nevertheless, is what you truly seek."

I had never thought of it quite that way. I admitted she was right. I had no intention of ever again setting foot in Keshavar. I would return westward, she would return eastward.

"And yet, dushizéh," I said, "we both want the same. Only in different places."

I must have spoken amiss. Her face clouded. After a moment, she answered:

"No, mirza, not the same. You hope to go back happily. I go to find what I fear most."

I pressed to know more. She said nothing after that.

We kept silently on our path for much of the day. Baksheesh still slept astride the donkey. I was beginning to believe more than ever that his tales were wild fancies. Our road, thus far, was hard-packed, well-trodden, and, in most parts, smooth. The hills on either side rose green with vegetation and groves of massive trees with wide-spreading branches. The air, light and fragrant, turned pleasantly cool as we went farther upland.

Late in the afternoon, Shira advised halting. It was not wise, she explained, to be on the road after nightfall. If we ate and slept now, we could start again at dawn and reach Marakand by midday.

We drew up at a clearing by the roadside. I shook Baksheesh awake. Yawning cavernously, he clambered off the donkey and blinked around.

"What a relief," he declared, scratching happily. "It's done wonders for my rheumatism. Stopping so soon? I could easily have gone a few leagues more."

Close by, a handful of travelers squatted on the ground. They had finished their meal, the small cook fire was dying to ashes. A couple of them, wrapped in hooded cloaks, had already stretched out to sleep.

A stocky man, thick-necked, with reddish hair cropped close to his skull, stood up and sauntered over to us. I dimly recognized him from the Joyful Garden of Happy Travelers.

"All friends here." He motioned for us to join them.

He gave Shira a good long glance and grinned at me. He had very bad teeth.

"Brought your girl, have you?" he said. "There's a comfort, eh? Well, fetch her along. We're good fellows. It's share and share alike with us."

"Not his girl." Shira's chin went up.

"Oh? What are you, then?" The trader gave a snorting laugh. "His slave?"

Shira looked squarely at him. "Nor that."

"So much the better. Come, I'll let you be mine."

He reached for her.

She swung up her arm. With all her might, she struck him backhanded across the face.

7

The trader grunted and fell back a step. One side of his face bloomed a dusky red; he was making every effort not to rub it. Blood started running from his nose and into his mouth. He spat it away.

"You half-breeds are the Devil's own spawn," he said between clenched teeth. "You'll pay me for that."

His hand went to the dagger in his sash. Behind him, his companions were on their feet.

I pushed Shira aside; more roughly than I intended, for she went stumbling. The man narrowed his eyes at me. He already had his dagger out. I drew the tulwar. I was giddy with terror and rage. Never a good combination. But my blood was up. I would have sliced him to ribbons where he stood. Had I known how. I pointed the tulwar at him.

My opponent looked me up and down. He bent his knees,

half crouching, and lightly tossed the dagger from one hand to the other.

"I'd only have cut her a little," he said. "Now you'll see if a half-breed wench is worth your life."

Baksheesh, meantime, was plucking my sleeve and wailing at the top of his voice: "I told you, I begged you not to draw your blade. You see what comes of it? Bloodshed! Murder!"

He rocked back and forth. "You bring woe and grief upon your head. O Prince of Fools! Supreme Idiot!"

I thought, at first, Baksheesh was addressing me. But, no, he had fixed his eyes on my adversary.

"Have lizards eaten your brains?" he cried. "Have you gone mad? Bade farewell to your senses? Pitiful lump of soon-to-be carrion, the vultures will pick your bones. Slack-jawed, scrofulous son of insane pigs, you should be groveling for mercy. Have you no idea who you're dealing with?"

The trader hesitated as Baksheesh pressed on: "This is Death Walks Abroad. Maker of Widows and Orphans. Terror of Travelers. Look your last on this world. Your next will be the fiery pits of Jehannum."

Baksheesh clutched at me. "O Mighty Warrior, I entreat, I implore you. Spare the life of this foolhardy worm."

One of the older traders had come up. "What's the quarrel? We want no trouble here."

"Trouble?" Baksheesh flung out. "Trouble is my master's

meat and drink. He kills to whet his appetite for breakfast. He spills blood to sauce his pilaf. Will you be rash enough to stand against him? He is Merciless Devastation. Tremble and behold al-Chooch!"

The traders exchanged uneasy glances. "I know nothing of this al-Chooch," the older one said, although with much uncertainty.

"Count yourself lucky," said Baksheesh. "Those who face him seldom live to tell the tale."

The red-headed trader shifted back and forth uncomfortably. He finally lowered his dagger.

"As he is wrathful, so is he compassionate," Baksheesh declared. "He forgives you in your benighted ignorance." Baksheesh motioned for me to sheathe the tulwar; which I did, glaring fiercely. Shira came beside me and held my arm.

"It pleases him to spare you," Baksheesh went on, as the traders, deciding caution to be the better course, inched away.

"Salaam, peace be upon you, O Prudent Ones," Baksheesh added cordially. "May your lives be long and happy, and your journey prosperous."

From the corner of his mouth, he muttered, "Get out of here, Excellence. Quick—but with dignity."

My blood was still up. I would have offered the retreating traders a few choice remarks of my own. Shira whispered to me to hold my tongue. We followed Baksheesh to the donkey and set off down the road again.

His rheumatism must have vanished. He stepped out so briskly we could hardly keep up with him. My anger likewise evaporated, but left me shaken; all the more as it sank in how narrow our escape had been.

Instead of slipping back and forth astride the donkey, I preferred walking with Shira. She was not as grateful as I might have wished.

"You told me you weren't a criminal or pirate," she said. "Now, mirza, I have to wonder: What kind of ferenghi are you? I think you may be a foolish one. You could have got yourself killed—and good-bye to your fortune and everything else."

"What would you have me do?" I said. "That pig insulted you—and would have done worse."

"Ah, mirza, mirza." She shook her head. "What do you know about worse?"

Not that much, I admitted. But enough. More than I needed.

"And, after all, dushizéh," I remarked, a little vexed, "you were the one who hit him first."

"A pig is a pig." She shrugged. "You should have let me deal with him. I have my own ways."

Then, almost under her breath, she added: "But you meant well, Carlo."

She pronounced it something like "Kharr-loh," and it was the first time she spoke my name. Looking back on it, I believe—to the extent that such a mystery can be reckoned with—yes, I believe this was the moment I fell in love with her.

But Baksheesh was calling us to join him in a sheltered space a little distance off the road. We unburdened the donkey. Shira found a stream nearby and watered the thirsty animal. I wanted some words with Baksheesh.

If I had risked my life, for all practical purposes he saved it. Having one's life saved is always a serious matter; one can never be eloquently thankful enough. I was at something of a loss what to say. Awkwardly, I did my best, adding that I would not forget.

"Be not concerned, Ocean of Gratitude," he said, modestly dismissing the subject. "I will take it on myself to remind you from time to time."

Shira had come back and begun preparing a light meal. Baksheesh had told me his assistant would be in charge of this duty. Even so, I suggested it was only right, at the end of a difficult day, for us to lend her a hand.

"Gladly," said Baksheesh, who had settled down with his back against a tree trunk. "You recall we agreed I am to be your camel-puller—once we have a camel, be sure I will pull it to your complete satisfaction. And, ordinarily, I would be happy to undertake a few small additional tasks. However, after such vigorous walking—as well as saving your life, Wonder of the World—my feet have a corn on every toe, bunions on top of bunions. With a few hours of complete rest—why—I'll dance all the way to Marakand. Tomorrow, be sure to wake me in time for breakfast. Then, off to an early start—"

"Better a late start," Shira put in. "Wait for those traders to pass us. If they think about it hard enough, they may decide they've been hoodwinked. Would you rather have them behind us or ahead of us?"

"You plucked the words from my mouth," said Baksheesh, caressing his feet. "I was just about to advise exactly that. As I would have told you, much wiser for us keeping an eye on them instead of them keeping an eye on us.

"By the way," he added, "I would heal faster if a little food, a morsel or two, could be brought to me. I should be able to assist you all the sooner."

"Let him be," Shira said, when I protested. "Your camel-puller at my elbow would be more trouble than help."

We left Baksheesh consoling his bunions. I had to admire how deftly Shira built a fire and set a pan to simmer on it. I supposed she had learned her skill, I said to her, at the Joyful Garden of Happy Travelers.

"No. My mother taught me; and my little brother, as well," she said. "My parents keep a caravanserai, a wayside inn east of Marakand. We make our living serving journeyers."

I began to see what she meant when she talked of travelers she knew. Some, as she said, all too well. As to be expected in a busy caravanserai. But how many? Dozens? Hundreds?

I resented—no, hated—every one of them. It pained me to imagine she had a past where I was not present.

I understood why she was anxious to make her way home. I did not understand why she had come so far from it.

Something else troubled me above all. I took her hand. She did not draw away.

Then the damned pan began scorching. She had to go and take it off the fire. And there was Baksheesh, leaning against his tree, like some overgrown fledgling, beak open, squawking to be fed.

I cursed the intrusive wretch. And his bunions, if he really had any. She went to tend that malingering faker—who had saved my life.

She did not sit beside me when she came back. She handed me a dish of food and stood by herself beyond the firelight.

I went to her. At the start of our journey she had said she needed to find what she feared the most. I had to ask what it was.

"Why is it your concern?" Then, after a time, she said, "Yes, I owe you that much."

I said she owed me nothing.

"I owe you, nonetheless." And so she told me.

8

"My father knew many tales," Shira said, "but there was one my little brother Kuchik and I best loved to hear. He told it always the same way:

"Once upon a time, fair-skinned, blue-eyed men from beyond the northern mountains stopped at a caravanserai to rest their camels and themselves.

"The mistress of the inn was a young woman of the Kirkassi folk who, long ago, had been a people of Cathai. There was a bold, handsome lad among the merchants; and this maiden was the most beautiful he had ever set eyes upon.

"But, next morning, the caravan made ready to leave for their own country, never to return again. The time came for the handsome lad to bid a sad farewell to the beautiful maiden.

"At this," Shira explained, "it was our part to cry 'No! No!' and make a great show of tearful protest. My father would pull a long, grim face and shake his head. It was, he told us, a cruel moment for the young lad.

"Then, my father would ask: How could he part from the most beautiful maiden in the world? And my mother, who always listened along with us, would blush and giggle. Ferenghi though he was, the lad had found his true home and his true love. But what else could he do? His companions were calling for him, impatient to be on their way.

"'And so the caravan moved on,' my father would say. He would pause a good many moments. Then he'd grin at us and add, 'He did not go with them.'

"We always cheered and clapped our hands, as we knew perfectly well the tale was of himself and my mother."

The caravanserai, as Shira described it, lay in a rare spot of greenery. The mountains shielded it from storms, it was well-watered by springs, a river flowed nearby. Travelers gladly broke their journey there.

"My mother and father worked to build the inn larger and more welcoming than it had ever been. It prospered. I grew up there and was happy."

I broke in to say I understood why she was eager to be home again.

Shira shook her head. Over this past year, she explained, fighting broke out between two warlords, each trying to win mastery of the best stretches of the road. The caravanserai was cut off from the main path and grew hard to reach. Fewer and fewer caravans stopped there. One by one, the stablemen and kitchen help left to find better work.

"In the end," Shira said, "the only one who stayed was our beloved housekeeper, Dashtani; and we kept the inn going as best we could.

"Some months ago, one caravan did come by. Close to a dozen traders, more guests than we had seen for a long time. Instead of camels, they had horses and pack mules. To me, this meant they had somehow skirted the fighting, avoided the worst reaches of the desert route, and followed a smoother road.

"They said nothing of what goods they bought or sold. That was not our business, what difference did it make to us? We were only too glad to have them. The caravan master, the one who seemed to be their leader, was a big, meaty-faced man with a coarse beard and quick eyes. Though he dressed like a Keshavari, he was a Westerner.

"He called himself 'Charkosh.' He was rough-spoken with his companions, but hearty and good-natured with us. He took a friendly interest in our caravanserai, so my father proudly showed him around, explaining and pointing out how we had built it up over the years. Charkosh did not tell us how long he and his comrades meant to stay; but he showed us money more than enough for anything they wanted.

"I had no cause to dislike him. But I did," Shira said. "I came to hate being around him. I felt his eyes always on me as

I went about my work. I kept this to myself and never spoke of it to my parents or Dashtani. They would, I knew, be angry at Charkosh. Only ill could come of it, so I let it go. He and his caravan would sooner or later be on their way.

"Charkosh had the habit of sitting late in the eating room. My father, as a good host, sat with him at his table while a couple of his companions lingered close by.

"One night, Charkosh sat up later than usual. At supper, he had told us he meant to leave the next morning. Several of the traders had already ridden ahead; a few others would stay another day or two. Charkosh himself, with the rest of his companions, would set off before dawn. I was relieved to hear that.

"I slept in a small room by the kitchen. What roused me were loud words between Charkosh and my father. I got up and crept to the doorway.

"'And I tell you, mirza,' Charkosh was insisting, 'you are starving your family to death. I see that for myself. Since I stopped here, how many other travelers have come? None. How many can you expect after I go? Likewise, none. Mirza, these are pinching times.'

"My father answered that times can change. Yes, we were going through lean days. But with a little patience, all would turn right again.

"'Patience?' said Charkosh. 'Tell me, mirza, can you eat patience for supper? I've passed caravanserais bigger and better than yours. What are they now? Empty shells. The sands have swallowed them up.

"'I want to help you,' he went on. 'You are a good, honest fellow. I like you. But clearly you have too many mouths to feed. We are men of the world, you and I. These things are done every day. Common practice. You know that. And you would still have the boy.

"'The girl will live a good life, better than any you could give. In a wealthy household, perhaps a nobleman's, with others like herself.'

"Charkosh took out a purse and set it on the table. 'I give you this much. Yes, of course, she'll fetch more on the open market. But, you understand, I must have a little profit. And consider my expenses.'

"My father had leaned forward. I did not catch all his words, but I had never seen such a look of rage on his face.

"'And so where do we stand?' said Charkosh. 'Have we a bargain? No? Are you sure? Ah, mirza, you will regret it.'

"It had taken a few moments for me to understand what Charkosh had wanted. I stood rigid, hardly believing what I had heard. Charkosh sighed and shrugged.

"'It is disheartening when people refuse to let themselves be helped,' he said. 'But, so be it.'

"He slid the purse back into his waistband. In the same motion, so quick my eyes could barely follow, he had a dagger in his hand.

"I cried out and ran to them. Charkosh kicked his bench aside and stood up. My father sat there, mouth open, staring bewildered, hands pressed against his breast. Blood was spreading over his shirtfront.

"I threw myself on Charkosh and tried to twist away the blade. He was gripping it too tightly. I bit into his wrist. I felt bone grating against my teeth. He cursed and struck at me. I clenched my jaw, he could not shake me loose.

"I had only a glimpse of my mother in her nightdress, Dashtani behind her, running down the stairs. I did not see my brother. Charkosh was beating at my face. His companions had jumped to their feet. One of them gave me a hard blow to the back of my head. That was the end of it."

I waited for her to keep on. She did not. She stood looking into the shadows. She had told me these things as if from a distance, as if they had happened long ago to someone else. If either of us was outraged and furious, it was myself.

This man Charkosh, a man I had never laid eyes on, had harmed her. I hated him for it. A total stranger had become, instantly and forever, my enemy. I was shaking with anger. Among all the wild notions galloping through my head, I wished him here in front of me. Baksheesh could not have held me back.

Shira was steadier than I. "And so," she said at last, "are the ones I love best alive? Or dead? I know nothing of what happened to them after that night. Could my father have survived his wound? Could my mother, my brother, my dear Dashtani have escaped? Have they been spared?

"If somehow they lived through it, I can only rejoice and be grateful. If they did not, I can only grieve for them. And swallow down my grief. One way or another, I have to know. To leave that question unanswered—part of my own life would be missing. Do you understand that?"

I said yes, I thought I did. Then I asked about Charkosh.

"I don't know." She shook her head. "Alive and in good health, I hope."

"What?" I said. "You wish him well?"

"Yes," she said. "Someday, with luck, I may see him again." At this, she brightened. "Oh, yes. Then I'll kill him."

I could hardly blame her. It did bring me up short, though, hearing the one I had given my heart to—as, indeed, I had—talk cheerfully about murdering somebody. She frightened me a little.

There had to be more to her account. I was not sure I wanted to find out, but I had to. So I asked her. Then half wished I hadn't.

After a time, she began again: "When my senses came back, I found myself roped to one of the pack mules. How long we had been on the road, I had no idea. By then, we must have gone some good distance from the inn. We halted once, as I remember. Charkosh lifted me off the mule and let me sit on the gravel.

"He made me eat a little food. I threw it up. He let me drink some water. I think he must have drugged it so I'd stay quiet.

I could not keep my eyes open. For a while, those last moments at the inn came to me again and again. Then, nothing.

"After some days—exactly how many I don't know, for I had lost track of time—I began feeling a little better. I was able to eat what I was given; my head cleared enough for me to think about how I would escape and make my way home. Also, I wanted very much to kill him. I thought about it a lot. I believe it kept up my strength more than food or water.

"By then, I was no longer thrown over the back of the mule, but allowed to sit astride. Though my hands were still tied, it was more comfortable. A couple of times a day when they stopped to rest, Charkosh unknotted the ropes so I could stretch my legs and rub my sore muscles.

"He spoke little to me, but his eyes were always on me, as they had been at the caravanserai. Once, close to night-fall, when I had lain down on the ground, he came and squatted beside me. From the look on his face, I guessed what he had in mind. Then he hesitated and seemed to think better of it.

"'Only a fool spoils his own merchandise before he sells it,' he said. Then he added, 'I'm doing you a favor. One day you'll thank me.'

"I spat at him and told him I'd kill him before that.

"I thought he would strike me. He only wiped his cheek and laughed:

"'So they all say.'

"Sometime after that, we caught up with his companions who had left the inn ahead of him. Along with them, I saw a dozen men or more and a few half-grown boys roped together in a straggling column. I knew for certain what I already suspected. His trade goods were slaves.

"I thought, at first, they had been taken by force, as I had been. I was wrong. They were kept apart from me; but, as I pieced together from talk among their guards, most came from villages whose people were glad enough to sell and be rid of them. Some were slow-witted, some had done one crime or another. Some had sold themselves to gain money for the sake of their families. As far as Charkosh was concerned, it was no more nor less than a matter of business."

I had heard nothing of such trade beyond a few words dropped here and there in Magenta. I was dismayed and not a little sickened, and I said as much to Shira.

"The cargo ships from Sidya have oars as well as sails," Shira answered. "Who plies the oars? Slaves, for the most part. It is not work that many take on willingly."

I remembered Baksheesh telling me, when we first met, that the world was a terrible place; and I would be astonished at what people did for money. And I was.

But—villagers selling their own folk? What kind of men were these?

"No better nor worse than any others, I would think," Shira said. "They do what comes to hand. And men like Charkosh find ways to profit from it," she added.

I was glad to say that in Magenta we had no part in such a business.

"Do you tell me your own merchants do not benefit one way or another?" she said. "It is just a little cleaner."

I had never thought of Uncle Evariste in that light. It annoyed me that I had no ready answer.

"And so we kept southward," Shira went on, "with Charkosh gathering more of his merchandise along the way. We soon had a good number. Nights, they slept on the ground, but Charkosh had put me in a small tent by myself. I was fed well enough, better than his own comrades. Not out of kindness. I realized he wanted me to make a good appearance. Like fattening a chicken before taking it to market. By then, I understood where we were going.

"Many towns are famous for the goods they sell. Some for their carpets, some for jade, some for handiwork in gold or silver. We were going to Akkar. I had heard travelers tell of it. Near the coast, close to Sidya. It was the biggest slave market in Keshavar.

"I thought, first, of trying to break free before we reached Akkar. I was no longer guarded all that closely. His men were busy watching their other prisoners, and Charkosh didn't seem greatly concerned with what I might do. Had I run off, they would have caught me before I went any distance. The countryside itself was the best and harshest of prisons.

"I knew nothing of the roads or trails in these parts. Even if I made good my escape, I would have been lost among the barren hills. Without food or water, I would surely have died. This I was determined not to do. So I bided my time until I saw what lay in store.

"After another week or so, we came into Akkar, a big jumble of a town. It was midday by then, hot and dusty. Wooden pens like sheepfolds lined all sides of the hard-packed earth of the marketplace. There seemed as many people in the square as in the pens, many haggling with the dealers but most looking on out of idle curiosity or amusement.

"Charkosh and his companions herded their merchandise into the largest of the enclosures, which I assumed was his customary place of business. I started to follow them. Charkosh held me back.

"'Did you think I'd have you muck in with those animals?' he said. 'No. You are already spoken for.'

"Seeing me uncertain about what he meant, he explained, with great satisfaction, that he had sent word to one of the local nobility. The matter had been settled in advance. We stood waiting while buyers and onlookers jostled around us and the dealers hawked their goods at the top of their voices.

"After some while, the crowd parted to make way for a band of horsemen. I counted four, and one riderless white mare. They dismounted. One of them approached us. He was richly dressed, long-armed, long-legged, without a trace of beard on his bony face. He was not himself the noble I expected, for Charkosh addressed him as 'mehmandár'—a chief steward's title. They spoke familiarly to each other. I supposed Charkosh had often dealt with him.

"Charkosh untied my hands to make me lift up my arms. I pulled away. He shrugged.

"'These half-breeds are stiff-necked,' he said. 'But so much the better, eh?'

"The mehmandár gestured at me with a twirling motion of his finger. I did not move.

"'Naughty, naughty,' he said to me. He and Charkosh laughed. The mehmandár added, 'His Excellency will find that entertaining.'

"He nodded approval and took a purse from his robes. Charkosh held out his cupped hands. The mehmandár began counting coins into them. A hush fell over the bystanders. These were not common trade-currency but gold pieces.

"'Continue,' said Charkosh as, at one point, the mehmandár stopped. 'The price agreed on.'

"'Mirza, you forget my commission,' the mehmandár said.

"'Mirza,' said Charkosh, 'your commission has already been taken into account, has it not?'

"'Ah—indeed, so it has,' the mehmandár said, with a sour twist of his lips.

"The onlookers stared as he grudgingly doled out one coin after another. Charkosh fixed his eyes on the mounting heap.

"'More yet,' he said. 'It doesn't please me to be stinted.'

"With his attention given to keeping close count of the price he demanded for me, I saw my best and only chance.

"I clenched my fists, thrust them under his outstretched hands, and struck upward.

"My sharp blow sent the coins flying into the air. The onlookers gasped in happy astonishment as gold pieces rained down on them.

"Charkosh, cursing, dropped to his knees to scoop up the scattered coins, as did the mehmandár. The guards left their mounts and ran to help their master. The bystanders scuffled among themselves to snatch all they could.

"Amid this mad scramble, I slipped through the crowd and jumped astride the mare. The startled animal bolted from the marketplace. Passersby stumbled out of her path. Street vendors flung aside their trays and baskets to escape the mare's hooves. She knew her way better than I did; I clung to her back as she plunged through narrow lanes and twisting alleys until we burst free of the town.

"Once on the road, I was able to calm the frightened mare and turn her northward to follow the coastline. I hoped to reach Sidya and lose myself there.

"I glanced back. Far behind, the guards, the mehmandár, and Charkosh himself must have recovered enough of the money and their wits to gallop after me.

"Sure they had seen me, I urged the mare off the road, sprang down, and sent her streaking into the uplands. I calculated they would follow until they saw she was without a rider. By then, I would be well on my way to Sidya.

"I slept in the bushes by day and kept in the shadows as I walked by night. In Sidya, I stopped at the first inn I came to and asked for work of any kind. Whatever his suspicions, the landlord did not question me. He was glad for an added pair of hands. Afraid Charkosh might somehow track me down, I thought it safer to dress in men's clothing, which the landlord was good enough to provide. The rest, you know."

Hearing her ordeal, I would gladly have taken her in my arms and comforted her. Exactly how, I was unsure. In any case, she did not appear to wish or need it. She had told me she owed me a debt. She seemed satisfied she had paid it.

"Kharr-loh," she said, "something more you should know. Understand it now. One day, I will leave you."

This set me on my heels. I began thinking she had a gift for putting me off balance. First, she let me believe she was a boy named Rabbit. Then, she reproached me for defending her.

She had let me hold her hand. And now she calmly told me she intended to leave me.

I asked what I considered a profoundly sensible question: "Why?"

"Because I must," she said. "Sooner or later, our ways have to part. You must do what you set out to do. As I will. I hope the best for both of us."

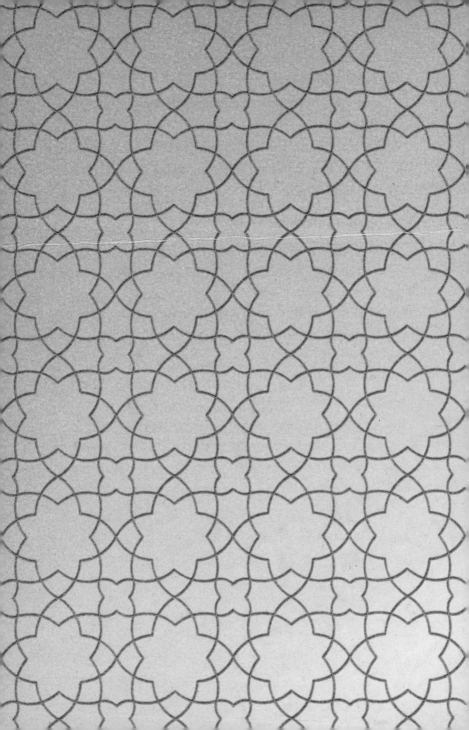

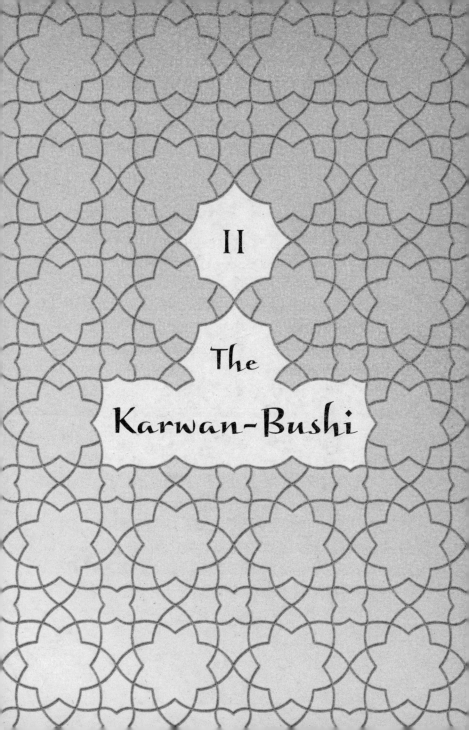

II

The
Karwan-Bushi

10

We came to Marakand the next afternoon. Late on purpose, as we waited for the traders to pass by. We watched them from behind the bushes. I wasn't sorry to see that redheaded ruffian wearing a bandage across his nose.

When sure they had outdistanced us, we set off again. Baksheesh had promised to dance all the way to Marakand; but he immediately began grieving over his bunions and settled himself on the donkey's back.

Shira and I walked ahead. We spoke little, and then only a few words about pack animals and the added provisions we needed.

Once, she bent closer to me and I had a feeling she was on the verge of telling me something important.

She didn't.

I had recovered, to some degree, from her flat statement that she meant to leave me—though it still felt a little as if she had gone at me, instead of Charkosh, with a carving knife.

First, she might change her mind. I had heard that girls did that from time to time.

Second, if she persisted in separating from us and making her own way home, I would seek her out no matter where her caravanserai was. I would, as soon as possible, show her my map to see if she could mark the location.

Everything, of course, depended on finding the treasure. With it, I could impress her with my new riches. I would offer costly gifts. My own appearance would be irresistible in garments more dazzling and luxurious than what I presently had on my back. I already saw myself in silken robes, gold-embroidered caftans, glittering rings, and bejeweled brooches. To complete the picture, I added a turban with a gem the size of a pigeon's egg. And—why not?—a peacock feather. Possibly several.

As for the treasure, I took for granted I would discover it. I had to. Of that, I grew more and more certain.

And so, as we passed through the great Western Gate of Marakand, I felt in better spirits than when we first set out.

Marakand—both Magenta and Sidya could fit into it with room to spare. Shira had spoken of towns famous for their different specialties. Marakand specialized in—everything.

"Behold, O Brightest Star in the Firmament," Baksheesh declared while we threaded our way along the busiest and most boisterous streets I had ever seen. "Here is all your heart desires—and your purse has money to pay for.

"Bazaars for sellers of cloth of silk, wool, goat hair. Bazaars for goldsmiths, silversmiths, pot-makers, leather workers—every trade you can imagine and some you've never heard of.

"And," he added, "the best and biggest Thieves' Market in the country. Excellent bargains. Should we require any, I shall take it on myself to obtain them.

"It is as I told you, Wondrous One. We could live here happily, if only you would take up some other line of work and forget—forgive me for calling it thus—the wildest of wild-goose chases."

I said that I wanted no further discussion. My mind was made up, more strongly than it had ever been. What we needed now was a place to stay until we could properly outfit ourselves and find a caravan to join.

"Only a suggestion." Baksheesh sighed in resignation. Pronouncing his feet temporarily healed, he climbed off the donkey. Shira and I followed.

To give him credit, he nosed out a small hostelry—a "khan," as it was called here—away from the most crowded quarters of the town. Pleasant and tidy, with a small courtyard, a fountain bubbling in the middle; clean-swept stables with an acceptably low number of flies. The rooms on the upper floor were tiny, more like pigeonholes for very large pigeons; but airy, almost cool.

Shira cast an experienced eye over the khan and nodded approval. We engaged three of the pigeonholes, and it was Shira, instead of Baksheesh, who expertly haggled the price with the landlord, one professional to another.

I was impatient to see about pack animals. And so we left the donkey to be fed and watered, and gave our baggage into the keeping of the porter.

Following his directions, we first made our way to the Great Souk, the central marketplace, a huge expanse with row on row of stalls and counters. The livestock market was a short distance beyond it. We began elbowing through the crowds. But then I hung back for a moment.

A rawboned, lanky figure stood at an open-fronted booth, really no more than four tent poles and a canvas top. Behind him hung a painted cloth backdrop. A piece of carpet lay on the ground; some coins had been thrown on it.

The man was even more raffish and ragged than Baksheesh, which was, in itself, remarkable. Yet something else caught at me. I could not put my finger on it, but it made me want to linger. Baksheesh tugged at my sleeve.

"Waste not a single one of the Pearls and Rubies of Your Precious Minutes," he urged. "Not on such a rogue and rascal. That ingrown toenail! That sack of noxious emanations!"

"A friend of yours?" I asked.

"Certainly not," Baksheesh protested. "But I know his kind, and they are all alike. Idlers! Layabouts! Lazy to the marrow of their bones. Notorious liars, without a grain of truth among all of them put together. Pay him no mind, it will only encourage him."

When I asked what sort of dreadful person this was, Baksheesh rolled up his eyes.

"Most Excellent But Unwary—heaven protect us, he is a public storyteller."

We had no such occupation in Magenta, apart from the usual scandalous gossip in the marketplace, and I loved a good story, so I was all the more curious.

This individual, meantime, had started whistling through his teeth, clapping his hands, and beckoning the onlookers to come closer. Shira seemed as intrigued as I, and we stepped to the front of the crowd, Baksheesh grumbling after us.

The public storyteller glanced around, shrewdly calculating if he had enough of an audience to make it worth his while. For one passing moment, he turned his sharp eyes full on me, looking me up and down as if taking my measure. For what?

"Hear and attend, O Best Beloved," he began; which, I guessed, was how these storytellers set about their business. And, to the best of my recollection, this was the tale he told:

THE WELL-DIGGER AND THE PRINCESS

Once, there was a young well-digger named Zameen. He was a little bit of a fool, but a most excellent well-digger; so good at his trade that the king himself hired Zameen to dig a splendid well in the royal park for guests to refresh themselves while admiring the gardens and orchards.

But something unfortunate happened to Zameen. The beautiful princess Aziza had the habit of strolling daily through the fragrance of the flowers and blossoming fruit trees. Zameen hardly dared speak to her beyond offering a respectful good morning. But the poor fellow had fallen hopelessly in love. And nothing could he do about it, for she was a princess and he no more than a well-digger.

One day, delving away and sighing as if his heart would burst, he unearthed a strange object: a large, long-necked green bottle stoppered by a seal covered with mysterious markings.

Zameen's eyes lit up and his jaw dropped, for he had heard that bottles like this always held a genie. Set free, the grateful genie would grant every wish.

So Zameen struggled mightily to uncork the bottle, but could not pry loose the seal. He gave it some good whacks with his shovel, but only broke the shovel.

"This could be a little harder than I thought," he said to himself.

He tucked the bottle under his arm and ran home to get stronger tools.

There he found a man sitting at ease in a corner. The unexpected visitor was dressed in ordinary garb, a turban wound neatly around his head, loose pantaloons, and slippers curling up at the toes.

The only unusual thing about him: He was so huge he took up nearly all the room.

"Peace be with you, Zameen," he said. "You may call me Radobarg—not my true name, but use it for the sake of convenience. I am a genie."

"If you're a genie," said Zameen, choking down his astonishment, "why aren't you in the bottle?"

"Why should I be?" said Radobarg. "Waste my time squeezed and cramped? I have better things to do. I buried that bottle for safekeeping while I ran a few errands. You happened to dig it up. So, if you please, give it here."

"Wait a minute," said Zameen. "What's in it?"

"A priceless substance, all the more precious because of its rarity," said the genie. "An elixir containing the concentrated distillation of the essence of common sense."

"What?" burst out Zameen. "That's all?"

"Nothing, I see, of interest to you," said Radobarg. "So hand it over and I'll be on my way."

"No." Zameen clutched the bottle protectively. "Of no value to me," he added craftily, "but obviously of great value to you. I'll give it back after you grant my wishes."

Radobarg's face darkened, his eyes flashed. "Pathetic little creature, do you think I couldn't squash you like a bug if I chose? Or"—the genie raised a huge hand—"simply wrest it away from you?

"But I'm a good-natured, easygoing genie. That's what you want? Very well, we have a bargain."

"I get three wishes?" said Zameen.

"Why only three? I'll be generous with you. Wish away. I'll tell you when to stop."

"First," Zameen declared, "I wish for vast wealth. Riches more than I can count—"

"Wait a moment," broke in Radobarg. "I'm beginning to suspect you are a person of limited imagination. Yes, I'll grant that. But where will you store it? In this wretched hovel? Let me suggest a suitable palace."

"Of course!" Zameen exclaimed. "I should have thought of that."

"But, then," Radobarg went on, "who's to clean it? Polish the silverware? Wash the golden dishes? Sweep the silken carpets?"

"Servants! Yes, an army of them!" cried Zameen. "And stables. A dozen camels and horses—"

"Why not hundreds?" the genie said. "Consider it done."

Zameen cocked a suspicious eye. "How do I know you'll keep your end of the bargain?"

"Genies always keep their word," said Radobarg. "More than can be said for you pitiful mortals."

At that, he took Zameen by the scruff of the neck; and, next thing Zameen knew, they were soaring high above the clouds. They landed, a moment later, amid the hills near Zameen's town. In a palace of glittering domes and towers, servants scurried everywhere. Magnificent horses and white racing camels filled the stables.

"You're an eyesore in a place like this," the genie said. "Here, now, have some fine clothing."

Zameen suddenly found himself arrayed in the richest silken robes and a turban with several peacock feathers. He was about to hand over the bottle, then hesitated.

"Uh—one thing more," he said. "Of a personal nature. I've been told I'm not a bad-looking fellow. But—can you do a little something for me in the way of, ah, improvement?"

Radobarg shrugged. He produced a mirror and passed it to Zameen, whose eyes popped at what he saw. He was handsomer than he ever dreamed. In addition, the genie had given him a gloriously curling mustache.

"A nice finishing touch, wouldn't you agree?" said Radobarg. "Now let's have that bottle."

Zameen gladly handed it over. By the time he left off admiring his reflection and twirling his mustache, the genie had vanished without so much as a salaam.

"At last," cried Zameen, "I'm in a position exalted enough to confess my love to Princess Aziza and ask for her hand."

He ordered his servants to load a dozen camels with riches from his limitless treasury. Zameen, on a magnificent steed, led the procession through the town, to the awe and wonder of the onlookers. He intended, as custom required, to ask her parents' permission to woo their daughter. At the palace, the chief steward greeted him with utmost courtesy.

"I am—uh, Prince Neemaz," announced Zameen. "I desire an audience with the king and queen."

Seeing the costly gifts he had brought, the chief steward immediately ushered him into the royal chambers.

"My dearest Prince Neemaz," said the king when Zameen declared his purpose, "I can tell at a glance you will make a perfect son-in-law."

"Go to our daughter," added the queen, after ordering the steward to notify Aziza. "I am certain she will eagerly receive you."

Attendants conducted him to Aziza's apartments. Zameen, sending ahead coffers of his choicest treasures, found her admiring the rings, bracelets, necklaces, and brooches set with precious gems.

"Prince Neemaz," she said, "I am flattered by your gifts, as any maiden would be. You are, beyond a doubt, the richest, handsomest of suitors; and your mustache is altogether captivating.

"However," she went on, "you come in vain. Though I dare not tell him, my heart belongs to another.

"My one true love is Zameen the well-digger."

11

Baksheesh kept nudging me, warning it was getting late and the best bargains in pack animals would be gone. Something about the storyteller puzzled me. Besides, I wanted to hear more. So did Shira.

"Is that all?" she said. "No better ending?"

If there was, I said, we'd never know. Thanks to Baksheesh.

"Of course you will, O Wonder of the Ages," he protested while we left the storyteller's booth behind us and crossed the Great Souk. "Any idiot can spin a tale of one sort or another. I prefer my own profession—whatever it may be at a given moment, it's surely more respectable than what that babbling blemish does to scrape a living.

"Do you want an ending? Here, I'll cobble one up for you straightaway. You'll see how easy it is.

"Very well, what happened was this. The well-digger,

what's-his-name, was overjoyed to know the princess secretly loved him; but in despair that she didn't recognize him.

"And so," said Baksheesh, "ah, umm, what did he do? What happened next?"

"How should I know?" I said. "You're the one telling the story."

"Ah, so I am, so I am," said Baksheesh. "What happened—he begged the princess to wait and promised he'd be back momentarily.

"He dashed out of her chamber and out of the palace as fast as he could. He jumped on his horse, for he meant to rush home, put on his everyday clothes, shave off his mustache—though he was fond of twirling it—and return as himself.

"So he went galloping down the street, impatient to straighten out the mess he'd put himself into.

"'I wish I'd never found that bottle,' he said. 'I wish I'd never got mixed up with that treacherous genie in the first place.'

"No sooner did he breathe those words than he was sitting in the dust. The magnificent horse had vanished from under him. He was in his same old rags. His mustache—gone.

"Delighted things were as usual, he climbed to his feet and ran to the palace. Everyone was milling around in confusion. His camels had disappeared, so had all the treasures he had brought. The chief steward was holding his head in consternation, the king and queen were bewildered as all the riches went up in a puff of smoke. And furious about it.

"The only one glad to see him was the princess. They flew joyfully into each other's arms, vowing eternal love. Her parents were horrified and outraged. They had lost a fortune and gained a well-digger.

"But there was nothing they could do. So what's-his-name and the princess went away together and lived more or less happily ever after.

"And there you have it," Baksheesh concluded. "You see how easy it was?"

But then, I asked, what about the palace in the hills?

"Why—it disappeared," said Baksheesh, "like everything else."

"And the well he was digging?" I said. "Did he ever finish it?"

"Who knows? Who cares?" Baksheesh said. "You wanted an ending? I gave you one."

I still wasn't altogether satisfied. Shira thought it good enough.

"Stories should all have happy endings," she said.

We really needed no instructions to find the livestock market. It was simply a matter of following our noses. And following the flies swarming toward our destination. They looked nearly as big as hummingbirds, and there were so many I thought they should have a bazaar of their own.

I had never seen a camel at point-blank range, let alone dozens all at the same time; nor heard worse honking and groaning since the day Uncle Evariste sprained his back.

"Pay no mind," Baksheesh told me, as I wondered if they were in the last throes of a painful and fatal illness. "They do it on purpose. Frauds! Fakers! Anything to escape working. What a world, where an honest man can't even trust an animal."

He stood gawking at them, shuffling his feet, scratching his chin—to such an extent that I had to ask if he truly understood the business of camel-pulling.

"You see a camel, so you pull it," he said. "What more to know? You can, O Paragon of Worthiness, have every confidence."

Shira had already gone into the pen. She walked briskly among the livestock, casting a shrewd eye on each one. She stopped now and then to study certain of them. She peered into their nostrils and mouths, felt their humps, appraised the size of their feet; she had them kneel and stand up again. Exchanging some words with the dealer, she chose two and led them out. The man followed, protesting as loudly as the camels, swearing he would rather stab himself in the heart than go bankrupt letting priceless stock go for a pittance.

"Pay him what I offered," Shira said aside to me. "When a camel-seller smiles, be wary. When he weeps, you know the price is fair."

"Yes," put in Baksheesh, "and when he says he's doing you a favor because he likes you, depart immediately."

Judging from the rivers of tears streaming down the dealer's cheeks and soaking his beard, Shira had struck an excellent bargain. I had previously dipped into my money belt, as if it were the Casa Galliardi bank, and withdrew what I guessed would be enough for any transaction. Shira haggled so well that I had a good bit left over.

Considering how much we had saved, she urged me to buy a horse. Depending on the nature of the roads, we would need one to ride or as a pack animal. Since she suggested it, of course I agreed. Only Baksheesh grumbled.

"You'll do so without my advice and guidance," he warned. "Horse-traders are worse than camel-sellers. Worse than public storytellers. They'll try to sell you a three-legged mule and tell you it's a rare and special breed. I want no part of them. They offend my sense of decency."

Leaving Baksheesh struggling with our camels—had they been able to speak, I felt sure their hawking and spitting were meant to insult him—we walked farther on to the horse market. There were a dozen or more mounts in varying states of disrepair. Shira's eyes lighted on a white mare.

The animal, I saw, had been hard-ridden and ill-fed; mane and tail hung in tangles; and it bore marks of the whip.

"That one," Shira said.

The horse-trader had been lounging by the railing. At her sign of interest, he brightened and came over with many welcoming salaams.

"Best of my whole string," he said. "Dushizéh, you have a keen eye for horseflesh."

"And for other things," Shira said. "Mirza, this mare has been stolen."

"What? I? A receiver of stolen goods?" he burst out. "You insult me! You insult all my ancestors! You come out of nowhere and accuse me, a man of supreme honesty—How dare you suggest such a thing?"

"Because I know," said Shira, "and I know because I stole her."

"Did you, indeed?" The horse-trader cocked an eye at her. "In that case, get out of here. I don't deal with thieves."

"How you came by her is none of my business," Shira went on. "But I can tell you this: She belongs to a rich and powerful nobleman. He will be most eager to have her back.

"But I like you, mirza. To keep you from harm, I mean to do you a favor. My friends and I will soon leave Marakand and take her away with us. Who's to know what became of her?

"Or," she added, "I need only pass along word that you have her. This mighty personage—his name does not concern you—is a man of wrath and vengeance. He and his retainers will gallop here to claim her. And you—your payment will be short and your punishment lengthy."

"I'm no fool," the horse-trader flung at her. "But you're a liar."

"Am I?" replied Shira. "Will you wager your head on that? Will you call me a liar when they tie you down, take out their knives, and begin peeling the hide off you one strip at a time? And, after that—"

"Take the accursed beast," blurted the horse-trader, whose face had gone dead white. "I give her to you. There is no such horse. She was never here. I never saw her. And I never want to see her again."

"No," Shira said. "On second thought, we would put ourselves too much at risk. Best for all—except you—if I send that message. Her owner may be generous enough to offer us a reward."

"Take her! I beg you!" The desperate horse-trader began pressing coins into Shira's hands. "For the sake of mercy!"

"If you insist," she said at last. "I hope, mirza, you will always think of us with gratitude."

With our little caravan in tow, and nearly as much money as when we started, we passed again through the Great Souk. I told Shira and Baksheesh to go on ahead, I would catch up with them.

I still had one thing to settle. I wanted to find the story-teller. I retraced my steps to where his booth had stood. The spot was empty.

I questioned the passersby, getting only shrugs and blank stares. Finally, I gave up. I elbowed my way out of the crowd, as perplexed as I had been when I stopped to listen to him.

Perhaps it was the appraising glance he had given me. Whatever it was, he had turned my thoughts to Magenta, to a sunny afternoon that now seemed years ago. And the map; Uncle Evariste throwing me out; and the start of the whole business that had brought me here.

He reminded me of the bookseller.

By the time I reached the khan, Shira and Baksheesh were already leading our caravan to the stables. That same instant, Baksheesh dropped the camels' ropes.

"Thief!" he burst out. "Desist! Skulking villain! Donkey-robber!"

12

Got you now, scrofulous serpent! You'll not escape. You'll rue the day I lay hands on you." Baksheesh, flailing his arms and shaking his fists, broke into a furious but circular dance that brought him no closer to the accused donkey-robber.

With Shira beside me, I ran to the intruder, who gave no indication of trying to escape or do anything else but stand observing us.

"Seize him, O Stern Chastiser of Evil-doers!" Baksheesh yelled. "Hold him down. He'll have me to deal with."

"Your friend appears upset," remarked the stranger: a short, stumpy man with features as sun-blackened and wrinkled as a Serrano raisin. Most of his head was bald and blistered, the rest of it fringed with grizzled hair floating in all directions. He turned a pair of twinkling gray eyes on me and nodded courteously.

"My name is Salamon," he offered. "Is this your donkey, messire? I assure you I had no intention of stealing this fine fellow. I was only admiring him. I've never met such a remarkable creature."

Baksheesh, meantime, had ventured to step closer. "A likely story. You dare claim you never saw a donkey before?"

"My goodness, thousands of them," Salamon replied. "But never this particular donkey. Look closely, each is different. This fellow's ears alone, for example. See the length of them? I must make a note of that. Amazing!"

Baksheesh snorted. "Well, Mirza Salamalek or whatever you say your name is, I've seen my own share of donkeys. I'd hardly call them amazing."

"How not?" said Salamon. "I find everything amazing. Sometimes amazingly good, sometimes amazingly bad. But amazing, nonetheless.

"You have camels, as well," he went on. "Alas, they are extremely unhappy."

"I suppose you talked to them," Baksheesh muttered, "and they told you."

"No need," said Salamon. "Look in their eyes. They are long-suffering creatures. Given a choice, they would prefer a different line of work.

"And this horse. A splendid steed in spite of her pitiful condition. She is of the bloodline of those famous Horses of the Wind. A marvelous animal. Stolen, of course."

Shira gave a laugh of surprise. "She is. What made you think so?"

"First, dushizéh," Salamon said, glancing kindly at Shira, "I don't reproach any of you. No, no, not in the slightest way. Your reasons, I'm sure, were excellent and no doubt of extreme urgency.

"However, my observations lead me to conclude the only way she came into your hands was by stealing. Since none of you could afford—"

"Wrong!" Baksheesh broke in, ignoring my motions for him to keep his mouth shut. "My master is an oasis of affluence."

"I'm so sorry to hear that." Salamon's face wrinkled. "What a burden it must be for him."

"And your observations, as you call them," declared Baksheesh, "are far off the mark."

"Do you think so?" Salamon said. He looked Baksheesh up and down. "You are sometimes a thief, frequently a liar. The list goes on and on. But you have a tender heart."

Baksheesh scornfully puffed out his cheeks. Salamon added: "Oh, yes. Your clothes, if you ever took them off, would stand up by themselves. But underneath them is a tender heart and loving nature. Whether you like it or not."

He glanced again at Shira. "You, dushizéh, know much, but there is one thing you turn away from knowing.

"And you? Easiest of all," he said to me. "You are searching for something."

That made me catch my breath. Baksheesh squinted suspiciously at him. "What's the trick?"

"Perfectly simple," replied Salamon, "if you call simplicity a trick. It's plain to see that you with so many—shall we say dubious—qualities must have at least one to make up for them."

He cast a shrewd eye on me. "And you, messire? Has ever there been a young man who was not seeking something?"

To Shira, he added: "Young women, and old, all know many things. And a few they wish they did not know."

"So, there is no mystery to it. Forgive me if I alarmed you," he said to me. "To demonstrate my good intentions, allow me to care for your animals. I can put that wonderful horse in the fine condition she deserves."

"A fair exchange," said Baksheesh. "I urge you to start immediately."

I thanked Salamon for his offer. I named each of us to him, asked if he was staying at the khan, and if he would take supper with us.

"As I eat little," he said, "the pleasure of your company will be sufficient refreshment. Yes, for the moment, I am stopping at the khan. I choose to occupy the stable. Sleep is such a boring waste of time, I seldom indulge in it. I find the company of animals calming and restful, which cannot be said for some of their owners."

Shira and Baksheesh went to arrange our evening meal. Baksheesh was still irked by the stranger's comments. "How dare he call me tenderhearted?" he muttered. "The old buzzard is clearly an idiot."

Curious, I stayed behind with Salamon. Although dressed in the usual traveler's garb, he carried no tulwar, dagger, nor any weapons I could see. Nor, for that matter, did he wear any boots.

"Nature is the best shoemaker," he said, noticing my puzzled glance. He balanced on one leg and, nimble as a boy, cocked up the other. He tapped the sole of his foot. I saw it to be thicker than a Magenta cobbler's toughest leather.

"This will last every bit as long as I do. Even longer," he said. "And it fits me perfectly."

There was something else I had in mind. We had been speaking trade-lingo; he had addressed me not as "mirza" but "messire," in what I heard as something of a Campanian accent. I inquired if Campania was his homeland and if he had been born there.

"Possibly," he said. "That far-from-momentous event took place so long ago, I have quite forgotten. Since then, I have been to more lands than I can count."

"You're obviously not one of them," I said, "but my uncle claims there are a great many fools in Campania."

"He is correct," Salamon answered. "An astonishing amount. More astonishing, it is exactly the same number as everywhere else. I would be hard-pressed to tell the difference between the fools of one country and the fools of another. Folly is our common bond."

Twilight was gathering. We walked to the khan. Thanks to Shira's professional advice, our landlord had laid out an excellent supper. However, Salamon hardly touched his food. Baksheesh did him the kindness of finishing all he left.

"Here, Salamanca, I'll show you tenderhearted," he said between mouthfuls. "How's this for a loving nature?"

For all his lack of appetite and absence of footwear, Salamon turned out to be the happiest of table companions. Despite his good nature, I guessed him to be a scholar, possibly once a schoolmaster; or, in any case, a person of high education. When I ventured to ask him about this, he chuckled.

"Good gracious, no," he said. "I've spent half my life learning whatever nonsense I was taught, and the other half trying to forget it."

In his turn, he inquired with keen interest what had brought me to Marakand. I was careful to tell only selected and harmless events: being dismissed from my uncle's establishment; the voyage to Sidya and my spectacular seasickness; that first encounter with Rabbit—in fact, the lovely dushizéh Shira. Salamon kept murmuring "Astonishing!" and "I shall make a note of that."

So, for casual table talk, I thought I was giving a fairly entertaining account—until Baksheesh broke in. "O Golden Tongue of Eloquence, allow me to mention: You're leaving out the best parts. My devoted diligence and invaluable assistance. And the treasure we're seeking."

I winced. With Baksheesh babbling on, I might as well have hired the Magenta town crier to spread the word.

"You search for treasure?" Salamon gave me a sorrowful look. "What a shame if you should find it.

"Your quest would be over," he said. "And then what? As if a fortune could make up for the bother of gaining it. No, no, my lad: The journey is the treasure."

He would have liked to know more; but Shira, seeing me squirm, turned the subject to his own destination.

"Eastward," he said. "Simply eastward."

At this, she bent closer, looking at him with keen interest. "I've heard travelers tell that secret wisdom can be discovered in the East."

"Did they find any?"

Shira laughed lightly. "None that I could notice."

"Of course not," said Salamon. "My dear dushizéh, I doubt there's greater wisdom in the East than anywhere else. Only people looking at the same things in a different way."

"Then, mirza," Shira said, "what do you seek?"

"Beyond Cathai," he answered, "some say there are vast oceans. Some say there may be islands, peninsulas, archipelagoes, whole continents. Some say there is nothing at all, and we end where we began."

"And you?" she said. "What do you expect?"

"I have no idea," Salamon said. "I only hope to find out for myself.

"Oh, yes," he added, "I shall definitely press on to the sea. As do we all, in our own fashion."

"Press away to your heart's content, Salmagundi," Baksheesh said. "I won't go a step farther than I have to."

13

We finished a pleasant supper. Salamon hurried to the stable. I wonder now if I had been given an inkling of what lay in store for all of us—would I have turned back then and there? Probably not. But how can anyone be sure? Much later, I talked about this with Salamon. I remember he blinked at me with amused tolerance, as if I had asked the silliest question in the world.

"Isn't there more than enough to occupy you for the present?" he said. "Why ever wish to know the future? It would only confuse you."

In any case, he made good on his offer to care for our animals. Over the next few days, while Baksheesh prowled the Thieves' Market to buy added gear, and Shira and I put our heads together calculating the provisions we needed, Salamon worked wonders.

Shira's horse—I considered it hers by right of prior theft—was in fine fettle again. The donkey's coat shone; it was no longer possible to count his ribs. The camels looked a little less despondent.

I had it in the back of my mind to ask Salamon to join us. Our caravan consisted only of myself; a camel-puller with the gift of vanishing like the storyteller's genie whenever he was needed; and a girl I was wordlessly in love with, who showed her affection by promising to leave me whenever it suited her. I had seen enough of Keshavar to realize this was not a powerful force to be reckoned with.

It surprised me when Baksheesh came out with the same idea. "I can overlook his insulting me," he said. "The old codger's tough as boiled mutton. He's got feet like iron. He eats next to nothing. He's good with animals, I'll give him that much. Not so good as myself, of course, but we can use the extra help. Above all, O Demanding One, it will allow me to devote more time and attention to your personal service."

Shira readily agreed. So did Salamon, who already seemed to have taken for granted he would go along with us. I still thought it wiser to be part of a larger company.

Baksheesh actually did something useful. He disappeared one morning after breakfast and came back with a big gray-haired fellow, hard-bitten, a man of his hands.

He was a caravan master—"karwan-bushi," as they called it here. He preferred simply to be addressed as "raïs," or captain. We all sat in the sunny courtyard of the khan and settled the price of attaching ourselves to his company.

"I'll be honest with you," he said, which immediately aroused my suspicions. As he went on, however, I sensed he was indeed telling the truth—and I liked it no better.

The raïs intended to head due east out of Marakand. I had privately studied my map whenever I could, so I practically knew it by heart. I pretty well understood what he was telling us.

It was, he explained, the smoothest stretch of road between here and the borders of Cathai. There were caravanserais at reasonable intervals, and frequent watering places. The surface suited camels and horses alike. It sounded better than I expected.

"I'll say straight out," he added, "I don't want to follow it. I can't vouch for your safety. More important, to put it bluntly, I can't vouch for my own or my people's.

"I've heard talk of robber bands," he said. "Well, true enough, there's always a few nipping at your flanks. Mostly a pitiful crew of starvelings. A nuisance more than anything. Like fleas on a dog. I'm used to that. I know how to deal with them.

"But word is they're getting bolder and there are more of them than usual. So far, no real trouble. But I have to take it into account. Mirza, I have a wife and young ones. Why should I go looking for a knife at my throat?"

Why, then, I asked, follow that particular path? My map had shown me a number of other ways that let him avoid it.

"The merchant travelers insist on it," the raïs said. "They won't go otherwise. The biggest towns, the best markets and trading centers lie along that route. The merchants count on making their fortunes by the time they're done. With the money they'll pay me, I'll take them to Jehannum and back.

"You, now," he went on, "you're an odd lot to be on the road. What's your line? Buying? Selling? Something other? You're not here for the scenery."

I wasn't so witless as to tell him I was hunting treasure. I left his question dangling unanswered.

He shrugged. "No concern of mine. Only understand this: Once on the way, you're under my command. You'll do as I say. I'm not happy to travel with a woman, but so be it. I require every able-bodied man to be well armed," he added to me, ignoring Baksheesh, who had suddenly blossomed out with a racking fit of coughing and wheezing.

"You can do me a service," he went on. "I need a donkey. The only ones I've seen here look as if they'd fall apart before they went thirty steps.

"I won't leave Marakand without one. I must have a donkey at the head of my caravan. Yours is in a better state than any I've seen.

"It is always done so," the raïs said, when I agreed but asked the reason. "Custom. Tradition. For good luck, some claim. I'm not so sure about that, it may be a pack of non-sense. Who knows? Why take a chance?"

I admit to a twinge of regret at leaving the khan. I had wanted to revisit the Great Souk and see if the storyteller had come back. In addition, the town was, all in all, a most agreeable, comfortable place. I even toyed briefly with the idea of convincing Shira to spend more time here. I let it go. The treasure kept goading me; and I doubted I could convince Shira of anything.

In the long run, it was beside the point. I never set foot in Marakand again.

We followed instructions the raïs had given, packed our gear, and loaded it onto the camels. At daybreak, we reported to a big, open area of hard-packed earth just beyond the town walls.

There, more camels than I had fingers to count them honked and bellowed. The camel-pullers yelled curses at the animals and one another. The merchant travelers milled around to no apparent purpose.

The raïs rode up on a bay mare. He looked us over, approved of my weapons. Salamon volunteered to walk beside the donkey. Baksheesh, meantime, was trying to persuade the camels to kneel and let us climb aboard. Shira had better success at it. Amid the crowd, I glimpsed one of the traders we had run into before Marakand.

I judged it wise to duck behind one of the camels. The man had already caught sight of me. I took a grip on my tulwar and stood my ground in front of him.

"Peace unto you, Chooch Mirza," he said. "Good fortune sends you to protect us."

I relaxed a little. Especially since he had put "mirza" after my name instead of before it, as if addressing one of great nobility.

"We are grateful," he went on. "We thank you for your mercy in sparing our lives."

"Only for the sake of your gray hairs," put in Baksheesh. "Be glad you still have a head to carry them."

I ventured to ask about my broken-nosed opponent. I didn't see him in the vicinity.

"That one?" said the trader. "He bears you a grudge; the girl, as well. But he is no longer with us. He goes his own way. Truth be told, I was happy to see the last of him.

"In Marakand, he took up with a merchant. A man of some wealth, so he appeared. A ferenghi—what was it he called himself? Oh, yes. Charkosh."

Shira had overheard us. She left off her work with the camel and went straight to the trader.

"You saw him?" she demanded. "Talked to him? Where did he go? When?"

The trader shrugged. "He stayed only a day or two at our khan. You know him, dushizéh?"

"After a fashion." Shira had that look I had seen before, and it more than halfway frightened me.

I added he was a notorious slave-dealer.

"As well may be," said the trader, "but he spoke nothing of that. The two of them had their heads together over some other matter of business. What it was, I do not know. Nor do I care to know. I can tell you no more than that."

The raïs, cantering along the gradually forming column, ordered us all to take our places. The trader, about to turn away, hesitated a moment.

"With all respect, Chooch Mirza," he said, bowing, "allow this humble person to dare ask one small question. I think of the day we met, and have always wondered, Why does a mighty warrior like your noble self journey with a donkey?"

"Childhood companions," Baksheesh put in. "They're inseparable."

14

The only way to enjoy a camel caravan, in my opinion, is to sleep through it. I was unable to do so. Baksheesh, I'm convinced, chose the camel with the more comfortable hump for himself; and promptly dozed off. I tried, first, riding astride; then with one leg crooked around the saddle horn. In both cases, it felt as if I were on the ridgepole of a high-pitched roof. Luckily, my lower quarters went numb and I felt nothing at all.

The raïs, in thanks for the use of our donkey, assigned us a place at the head of the column. Far better than the tail, where you eat and breathe the dust and whatever else from all the animals ahead of you. We had a good view of the rear end of the leading camel: decked out—by custom, I supposed—in festive finery with embroidered draperies, ribbons, tassels, and a little brass bell swinging from the harness.

The raïs had hired outriders, armed guards to patrol the vicinity, alert for any sign of robber bands. They seemed as brutal and ruffianly as any robbers I could imagine. I was glad of that. After all, if you need a watchdog, best get yourself a vicious mastiff, not one of those fluffy little pets that some of our Magenta ladies favored. A few of the merchants rode their own horses. Shira walked beside her mare. Salamon and the donkey stepped out in a steady pace, the donkey more cheerful than I had ever seen him.

However, apart from the crunch of the camels' feet over the shale and gravel, and the endless tinkle-tinkle of that bell, the caravan was mostly silent. What was there to talk about? Hardly a setting for spirited conversation.

We halted once, and briefly, at a small oasis: the only spot of bright green in a trough between drab gray hills and scrubby woodlands. The raïs ordered us to move on until we reached a caravanserai.

We came to one before dusk. But it was deserted, already crumbling into ruins. The raïs was grimly disappointed though not surprised. It often happened, he explained, that caravanserais, even whole villages, would spring up, flourish for a time; then, for whatever reasons, fall into decay. Here, at least, we could shelter against the night chill. In what had been a courtyard stood a well of scummy water. It looked only mildly venomous.

Despite my screaming muscles, I was happy to be together with our little group. Baksheesh made a few sketchy gestures at unloading the camels; then quickly gave it up, wailing that his lumbago had viciously assaulted him. Salamon, as bright and unwilted at the end of the day as he had been at the start, offered to put his joints right.

"Hands off me, Saladino. You'll do more harm than good," he grumbled. "I'll stretch out for a bit. I prefer to let nature take its course."

As my chief camel-puller, I had yet to see him do anything resembling pulling a camel. So the rest of us tended to the animals. We sat, then, a little while on one of the stone slabs circling the court. Shira, restless, wanted to seek out the trader, who may have overlooked some scrap of information about Charkosh and his whereabouts.

I urged against it. She wasn't listening. I suspected what she had in mind. Given half a chance, I believe she would have gone after him; probably with our best carving knife. Her dark mood puzzled Salamon until I spoke aside and briefly told him her reasons.

"Oh, dushizéh, that would be foolish," he said to her, "and you do not have the look of a fool."

"My business, not yours. You know nothing—" She put her hands over her face. "I'm sorry. I didn't mean that. Forgive me."

"Most certainly, I will not." Salamon smiled fondly. "No need. Why ask forgiveness when you speak truth? I know nothing. Good heavens, I can hardly remember how much I've forgotten. The older I get, the less I'm sure of. I hope to end up sure of nothing at all.

"I only suggest to you: Will you dwell on killing this man? You wish revenge? If you do, he has already killed you by slow poison. So, let it go. Why waste your time? His life will see to his death."

Shira did not answer. Whether she took his words to heart, I had no idea. Then again, I usually had no idea what she was thinking.

I did gain some skill in staying perched on my camel. What I lost was my sense of time. Caravanserais were few, far between, and all so much alike it might as well have been the same one again and again. We most often halted at a small oasis or meager watering place. When I slept, I dreamed I was still riding in the caravan; awake, I daydreamed I was asleep. Mornings and nights blurred into one another. As best I can reckon, we had been some three weeks out of Marakand.

That was when the butchery began.

I understood, later, how it came about. By then, it made no difference.

All that day, the raïs had been pressing us hard to speed our pace. We were going through a long, narrow stretch of road with steep slopes and dense woodlands on either side. The raïs was edgy. This would be the most likely spot for robbers to attack. Once the road widened again, we all breathed easier. Best yet, we soon reached a large oasis. Lush vegetation fringed a shimmering pool; and even banks of flowers a lot sweeter smelling than we were.

It was some while before nightfall, only the faintest streaks of purple and pink showed in the sky. We were all grateful for the chance to rest. Salamon and the donkey joined us, both in the best of spirits.

We began unloading our camels. The tail end of the caravan had not yet come to the oasis. I heard a terrible ruckus. Men on shaggy little mountain-bred ponies were riding full tilt into the rear of the column. How many I couldn't tell, I only caught a glimpse. The raïs may have expected pitiful starvelings. These looked fairly well armed with lances and long-bladed swords.

The pack animals were shrieking. The bandits, I learned later, were trying to blind or maim them, cut the legs from under them, and rifle whatever valuables came to hand.

Our guards galloped to their defense. Whatever the raïs paid them, they more than earned it. They were ferocious, chopping and slashing with heavy, upcurving scimitars. But the robbers had been clever. This attack was only to lure the guards from the main body of the caravan.

There had been no sign of bandits along the way. They were already here.

They had been waiting for us. Now they burst out of the

shrubbery, whooping and howling. A moment later they were among us. The only thing I clearly remember was taking hold of Shira and sending her into the arms of Baksheesh. I shouted at him to get her out of there. She struggled with him. Had he let go, I believe she would have gone hand to hand against the robbers. Salamon ran to Baksheesh. Between them, they pulled her away. That was the last I saw of them.

These things happened quickly. They seemed to go on forever. I was being shoved, stabbed at, battered back and forth. I struck out blindly, without even a chance to draw my dagger or tulwar. I thought it would never stop.

I have no idea exactly when the tide turned in our favor. The bandits surprised us. We surprised them. They never expected us to fight back so fiercely. I would see two or three traders and camel-pullers fling themselves against a robber, drag him down, and kill him on the ground. And so it went. At the end, our attackers lost heart. They broke and ran.

And I did one of the stupidest things in my life.

I stole Shira's horse.

The raïs had a knife cut across his face. He was very angry. He kept shouting at us to go after them, run them down, damned if he'd let those pigs' offspring get away. I heartily agreed. Was I outraged because Shira could have been killed? And the rest of us, as well? Our goods ransacked? Yes, it was all of that. And stupidity, of course. Lunacy as much as anything. At the moment, it seemed the right thing to do.

The white mare, untroubled by the fighting, stood at the edge of the pool, cropping the grass. I ran and jumped astride.

She startled and tossed her head. I kicked my heels against her flanks. She plunged full stretch through the ruck of traders and camel-pullers, nearly leaving me straddling empty air.

I got only as far as the middle of the road. The mare, by then, realized she had an idiot stranger on her back. She halted, reared, and sent me flying over her hindquarters. I sprawled to the gravel. She snorted and ambled away to the caravan.

My fall knocked the wind out of me. I sat up and looked around. I saw none of the bandits on their ponies. The ones who had attacked us on foot were scrambling up the slopes and disappearing into the underbrush. I staggered to my feet and set after them, trying to run and catch my breath at the same time.

Surprisingly, I ended up capturing one. Accidentally. I had plunged into the brush, making little headway. If his foot hadn't slipped, if he hadn't stumbled, he would easily have escaped. Instead, he came crashing down on top of me.

I didn't get a good look at him. Only the quick impression that he was about my size. Maybe a year or two younger, he had no more than the peach fuzz of a hopeful beard. A lanky boy. But he was strong. All I could do was grapple with him and hang on while he kicked at me and thrashed about.

He bit me on the side of my face. I flinched but kept my grip on him. I managed to heave him clear of the bushes and brambles.

We went rolling down the slope to the roadside. I still hung on. He struggled to get his arms free. One of our guards rode up. He slid off his horse, walked over, and kicked the boy in the head, which calmed him down.

I untangled myself. The guard bent, set a knee on the captive's neck, and deftly roped his hands behind his back. I stood up, very unsteady.

"Well done," the guard said to me. "You go on, I'll take care of this." He grinned. "That's what they pay me for."

I went to the caravan. The oasis was a mess. Some of the baggage had been slashed open and rifled. Clothing and odds and ends of equipment were scattered over the grass. The travelers, cursing and complaining, sorted through their goods.

Shira saw me right away and came over. She was furious. I never imagined she knew words like that. I couldn't decide if she was upset because I risked my life or because I had temporarily stolen her horse. Probably the horse. I wasn't listening closely. The bite on my face hurt. I was in no frame of mind to be yelled at by anybody. Shira least of all.

I sighted Baksheesh and Salamon. Both looked unharmed; our animals likewise. Closer to the tail end of the caravan, some of the pack animals had been badly maimed. The camel-pullers had to go and put them out of their misery.

The raïs called us around him. His wound had stiffened and puckered up a corner of his mouth. He gave a quick tally of our damages: one camel-puller heavily wounded; two, lightly. Three merchants dead, including the trader who had addressed me so respectfully as "Chooch Mirza." I saw him stretched on the ground. His throat had been cut; his caftan was sopping red. The raïs ordered them buried a little way from the oasis.

There remained the matter of the bandits. Three others had been caught in addition to the one who tumbled into me. Hands tied, they squatted on the gravel, saying nothing. Their faces were hard-set, without expression. Except for the youngest, who looked more boy than man. His eyes were so wide open the whites showed all around.

"Put them up." The raïs motioned to the guards standing, arms folded, behind them. He pointed to the far side of the road. The guards hauled their charges to their feet and herded them to the spot the raïs indicated. No one hurried. It was almost leisurely.

A couple of the camel-pullers, meantime, had found tent poles and whittled points at the ends. Twilight was coming on. The air itself seemed thick and blue. Somebody lit torches and carried them over so the guards could see better what they were doing.

"If they're careful about it," one of the traders remarked to me, "those pigs should last a good while."

I didn't know what he meant. I wanted to join Shira, who had gone to Baksheesh and Salamon. But I watched in spite of myself. Some of the traders broke out provisions and started cooking supper. A handful of merchants and camel-pullers strolled across the road. They stood around, observing, making comments, joking among themselves.

The guards flung their captives to the ground. One turned stubborn at the end, kicking up his heels, flailing his legs back and forth. The guards ignored this and went about their business.

I had to turn away. I pressed my hands over my mouth and ran through the camp as fast as I could. I wanted to go into the bushes at the far side of the pool. I didn't get quite that far. I doubled over and threw up. Several times.

Shira had followed me. I gestured for her to go away. I didn't want her near me. I stank too much. My stomach kept on heaving. I went past the fringe of shrubbery. Far enough to be out of earshot of the screaming.

I still heard it inside my head. I sat down. I thought I was going to throw up again, but there was nothing left. At first, I didn't notice Salamon beside me.

He asked if I was all right.

I said no, I wasn't.

"You will be," he said. "More or less. Sooner or later."

"There was one of them. A boy." I told him about it. I hadn't known anything like this would happen. But I had a hand in it. I killed him as surely as if I had stabbed him with a knife.

"I'm afraid that's true," Salamon said.

I thought he could have come up with something better than that. It did not cheer me.

"What shall I do?" I asked.

"Anything you choose," he said. "Only one thing you can't do, nor can anyone: Undo what you've done."

"Does it matter?" I wondered. "Why care one way or another? Why not run like a madman with all the other madmen?"

"The world has trouble enough as it is," he said. "So why would you add to its miseries?"

"The raïs is really the one who killed him," I said after a time. "Out of hand. Just like that. Judge and executioner. He condemned them all to death."

"And you," Salamon said, "have been condemned to life."

Later, he went back to tend our animals. I still sat, knees against my chest, eyes tight shut, hands over my ears.

I decided to sit there—how long? Forever?

The body makes its own decisions.

Mine slept.

16

In the morning, I got up and went to the oasis. It was going to be a perfectly beautiful day; cool and clear, the sky without a single cloud. Dew filmed the grass. At the pool, I splashed water on my face. I glimpsed my reflection. I had trouble recognizing myself. Shira once raised the question: Was I a criminal or a pirate? I can only say that if I had seen someone who looked as I did, lurking around the port of Magenta, I would have gone briskly in the opposite direction.

Everybody was awake and stirring. The campsite had been tidied. I did not dare glance across the road. I wanted to find Shira. Wherever I went, she was someplace else. I suspected she was avoiding me.

The raïs, on horseback, ordered us all to gather around. His face was gray; the knife wound had turned black and crusted over. He seemed a lot older than when I first met him. He motioned for us to be quiet.

"Listen," he said. "I'm not a coward. Not a fool, either. How do I know those devils won't get themselves together and come at us again? Tonight? Tomorrow? Here? Or down the road?"

He held up a long pole, nearly twice my height; a heavy spear with an ax blade set on one side of it, an ugly looking hook on the other. I would have called it something like a halberd, the kind our night watch carried in Magenta.

"Where did they get this?" he said. "Stolen somewhere, of course. Do they have any more of them? Probably not. If they did, they'd have used them. And most of us would be missing a few arms, legs, and heads. Are there still more robber bands? Bigger? Stronger? I don't know. All I know is I don't like the smell around here.

"What it comes down to is this," he said. "If we go on, I can't promise you'll be safe. So I'm not taking you any farther. The caravan has to turn back." He grimaced. "I won't swear I'll even get you to Marakand again."

Some of the travelers grumbled a little, more for the sake of grumbling than anything else. After they thought it over, and had a good look at that halberd, they grudgingly admitted he was right. I really believe they were glad.

I know that I was. My treasure hunt had started badly and left a sour taste in my mouth. I needed to make other plans and follow some different road.

"Get your people ready," the raïs said to me. "The sooner away, the better."

Salamon had already bridled the donkey. I told Baksheesh to pack up and load the camels. He did not protest. He said never a word about his lumbago, his knees, bunions, or anything else. I feared he might be sick. He was not. He was overjoyed, practically hugging himself with delight.

"I hasten to obey your command, O Repository of Wisdom," he said. "Only forgive me for mentioning it, but had you listened to me in the first place, we'd not be here at all. The last thing in the world I wish, Gracious Worthiness, is to see you deceased. The other last thing is to see myself in that unhappy condition. I suppose," he added to Salamon, "that includes you."

"You show concern for a fellow creature," said Salamon. "I knew you had an affectionate nature."

"Profound affection," said Baksheesh, "for my own skin. Besides, I don't want to tempt fate. You should have sense enough to be concerned for yours."

"Yes, up to a point," Salamon replied. "Death is an inconvenience, forced upon us whether we like it or not. Fate is something we make for ourselves. In any case, I find other things more enjoyable to contemplate."

"Contemplate to your heart's content, Scaramuzzo," Baksheesh said. "Meantime, you could lend me a hand with the camels."

Shira had finished saddling the mare. We had hardly spoken to each other since the night before. She gave me no more than a glance when I walked over to her. She did not appear too happy with the world in general and myself in particular. Apart from that, I thought she looked marvelous.

"You look awful," she said.

I told her I knew that. I added I was sorry about the horse.

She began stowing things into her bag. "You should be."

She did not continue the conversation. I wondered if I had been sorry enough.

"I'm really very sorry," I said. "Really. Very sorry."

"I'm sure you are," she said.

"It's going to be all right." I told her the raïs knew what he was doing. It was for the best. We'd stay in Marakand a little while, then start over. It was the only sensible thing.

"Do as you please." She tied up the bag and roped it behind the saddle. "It's your caravan."

"I suppose it is," I said. "I hadn't thought of it that way."

She pressed her lips tight and tinkered with the harness. More than necessary. Finally, she turned to me. If she hadn't been so annoyed, I would have said she seemed forlorn.

"Kharr-loh," she said, "I'm leaving you."

17

I told you I would," she said. "I told you from the beginning."

She really did have a gift for putting me off balance. This time, her face held a fragile expression I hadn't seen before.

"Well," I said, after a couple of moments, "you mentioned something like that."

"I didn't tell you I wanted to," she said. "I've come this far. I have to keep on. I'm going home."

"So you're leaving me?" I said. "But I'm not leaving you."

"That's your choice," she said. "Your decision."

"My caravan, too," I said. "I'd better tell the others."

She nodded. "Do that."

Salamon took the news happily.

"Marvelous," he said. "Though not surprising. I'd be surprised had you done otherwise. If it suits you, I'll come along. You'll need someone to tend the donkey."

Baksheesh was another matter. When he heard what I intended, he carried on as expected. He begged, he pleaded, he warned of every possible disaster. He whined and sniveled by turn and at the same time.

"Woe and misery!" he wailed. "Looking for treasure is one thing. Looking for trouble, that's something else."

I told him never mind, he'd be going with the raïs.

"You think that's any better?" He stopped short. "No. I can't do that. I gave you my word—"

"So you did, and I accepted it," I said. "Now I release you from it. Go. You're free to do as you please."

"O Liberating Benefactor," he protested, "Ocean of Generosity, I must decline. There is a difficulty.

"While I was patronizing the Thieves' Market—on your behalf and for your benefit, of course—a small misunderstanding arose. Certain things were said and done, accusations—altogether false—were made. Threats were expressed, suggestions offered. Something along the lines of if I had any interest in staying alive I'd best not set foot there again."

"You never told me anything like that happened," I said.

"Didn't I?" said Baksheesh. "Ah. I neglected to mention it? Yes, it slipped my mind. I forgot. I didn't want to upset you. I let it pass. I'm just now reminded—"

"My dear friend," put in Salamon, "I say this with all respect and affection: You are a liar."

"I'm an innocent victim of circumstance." Baksheesh drew himself up indignantly. "I'm stuck with the lot of you, like it or not. And I don't like it, never did, never will."

"I think you'd rather be fried in oil than admit it," Salamon said, "but I do believe you may have had a twinge of decency."

"A lot you know," Baksheesh retorted. "Do me a kindness, Savonarola. Keep your nonsense to yourself."

I took my leave of the raïs. He shook his head, much concerned.

"Go off on your own?" he said. "Then you're truly a fool. Of highest quality. If you were a diamond, you'd be flawless. The girl has something to do with it, I'll be bound. There's no room in your head for common sense. Ah, well, that's your business. Peace unto you. And I thank you for the loan of your donkey."

I never knew if he reached home safely.

As Shira said, it was my caravan. Though it had never dawned on me that I might actually carry some responsibility for it. In Magenta, I had imagined myself boldly leading an expedition that brought us happily to a fortune. I did not reckon on obstreperous camels belching and spitting on me. Or on keeping a constant eye on Baksheesh, who worked extremely hard at doing as little as possible. Or on watching over Salamon, who tended to wander off and marvel at some strange rock formation or odd specimen of plant. I certainly had never looked forward to the fine grit that seeped into every garment down to my underclothes. Not to mention blisters where blisters had no right to be.

And Shira—yes, of course, she understood the network of roads and trails and knew more than I ever would. Even so, in time it pleased me to believe—or, at least, pretend—that I became an almost acceptable karwan-bushi. Anyway, I liked being an imitation karwan-bushi better than being a genuine chooch.

However, on the day we parted from the caravan survivors, I wanted only to get away from the place as fast as possible. The raïs had ordered the bodies left to rot on their poles as a warning to other gangs of bandits.

Bound in awkward, angular postures, they were dead by now. Or so I hoped. I still had to turn my eyes from them. I had no stomach for the sight. From what I accidentally glimpsed, they no longer looked like people. They gave me nightmares for a long time after.

What puzzled and troubled me somewhat: We met no caravans coming from the east. The road stretched empty and bleak. We did find watering places; on occasion, a little oasis. Caravanserais were few, not especially happy or welcoming.

The last one, where we hoped to shelter and replenish our dwindling store of provisions, tried to turn us away.

Shira had ridden on ahead. She dismounted and stopped at the entrance. When we joined her, I saw that a heavy chain had been drawn across the gateway. This, as I had learned, was done at night to bar unwanted arrivals. It was still broad daylight. Shira, frowning, turned to me.

"He says they're full."

"Full of what?" Baksheesh muttered. "Not travelers. We haven't seen any for days."

"Quite astonishing," Salamon said, undismayed. "I've never heard of such a thing. I must make a note of that."

Shira tried to persuade the porter to let us in, assuring him we had money to pay for all we wanted. By now, the innkeeper himself had appeared.

"Your money's worthless here," he said. "Food and lodging? I have neither."

The best he would do, as he finally agreed, was to let our animals drink and let us fill our water bags at the well. He could offer no more than that. We would have to keep on our way.

I did not understand this. Every caravanserai I had seen was near a town or village that supplied meat and vegetables and whatever else was needed. When I asked him about it, his face darkened.

"What village?" he said. "Raïs, it's here."

He ordered the porter to lower the chain. We went into the courtyard.

I had never seen so much misery in such a small space. Heaps of rags and refuse littered the courtyard and the arcades that circled it. When I looked closer, I realized these were men and women, their young ones and babes in arms. They squatted dazed and silent. I could scarcely tell the difference between them and their piles of belongings.

"There's the village. The ones who lived through it." He spread his hands. "I took them in. What else could I do?"

"The tribes are at each other's throats again," he went on, seeing my confusion. "Kajiks. Karakits. Sworn enemies for generations. Who knows why? It has always been so.

"This time, the worst. Because of the fire. The Kajik warlord and his men rode in and burned half the village. No one had seen anything like it. They could not put out the flames. Water only spread the blaze. The ones who did not escape—their ashes still smolder."

"So these folk are Karakits?" I asked.

"No," he said. "Nor Kajiks. They are Aftabis, as I am. They have no quarrel with either side. Indeed, next day, the Karakits attacked and set fire to what was left. Why? So neither tribe could have it.

"They have been here three days now. How long can I keep them?" he went on, as we picked our way through the bundles of clothing and household goods to reach the watering troughs. "My provisions are exhausted. Shall we all starve together? And who knows if one warlord or the other will take it into his head to burn down my caravanserai for the joy of watching it go up in smoke?

"Fill your water bags, raïs, and go your way," he said. "Peace be with you. It is surely not with us."

18

I had made up my mind to put off my own search and stay with Shira until she reached home safely. The treasure, wherever it was, had been sitting there for who knows how long. It could sit a little longer.

As I recalled from my map, two or three days' journey should bring us to a road crossing this one. We needed only to follow it southward. Simple enough. I should have known nothing in Keshavar is simple.

No sooner had we set foot outside the caravanserai than a ragged column of folk from yet another village arrived, pleading for shelter. When they saw which way we were heading, they warned us that fighting had spread all along the road. They were carrying their lives on their backs. I feared we might be taking our lives in our hands.

The last thing in the world I wanted was to run afoul of battle-drunken Kajiks and Karakits. In case Shira was any way tempted to risk it and keep on, I mentioned what I judged a certainty: "If we fall in with either side, whatever else they do to us, one thing's sure. They'll take your horse."

That convinced her.

Our best course, then, was to get off this accursed road as soon as possible. I found a way to do it. Not far from the caravanserai, we came upon a narrow trail. While hardly an inviting path, at least it bore southward. My map hadn't shown it, but I wasn't going to quibble over small details. I proposed following it. Sooner or later, it would have to lead us to one of the better-traveled roadways. There would surely be way stations, towns, or trading centers.

"And if not?" said Baksheesh.

"Then," I said, "I'll think of something else."

"Of course you will, O Intrepid One," he muttered. "That's what worries me."

Salamon offered to go ahead by himself, see what we had to deal with, then come back and report what he found. I urged against it. I did not want us to be separated. Further, should anyone scout ahead, it was the duty of the karwan-bushi. If I had assumed the title, I should try to earn it.

Shira, without waiting for us to chew over the question, had already gone a little distance through the underbrush.

"The animals can manage well enough," she said when she rejoined us. "It's passable. Others have gone this way."

"You call that good news?" Baksheesh put in. "What others? I'd rather nobody was here before. If you ask me, this is just the sort of hole-and-corner nest for bandits and who knows what else."

I wished he hadn't said that.

"On the other hand," he went on, "I've never met a Kajik, let alone a Karakit. I'm sure their mothers love them, but I shall strive hard to live without that pleasure.

"To make up for the disappointment," he added, "I do find one attractive aspect about this pitiful excuse for a road."

"Excellent. I'm gratified to hear you say so," Salamon told him. "Your true nature is definitely blossoming. In spite of difficult circumstances, you are able to appreciate what is interesting and enjoyable."

"Right you are, old Salazar," replied Baksheesh. "What I'll enjoy most about this dismal path: It's downhill."

As karwan-bushi of what had to be the smallest caravan in Keshavar, I learned two great but simple truths. First, a caravan goes no faster than its slowest camel. And, second, the slowest camel goes no faster than its most reluctant camel-puller.

Shira's judgment had been correct. The trail was passable, though barely so. Our donkey was sure-footed, Shira's mare likewise. The camels trudged on, resigned to yet another misery added to their daily lives. Baksheesh, however, constantly lagged behind. Also, during the time we spent picking our way down the tangled slope, he left off grumbling only when he was asleep. At least there were no lurking robbers. I was glad of that. But I half wished we had taken our chances with the Kajiks and Karakits.

We reached the valley floor around noon. Was it the second or third day of our downward climb? I can't be certain. I had come to calculate the difference between day and night according to whether Baksheesh was complaining or snoring.

Here, a wide corridor of coarse sand stretched along the edge of high, jagged hills. I had never seen such a vast amount of nothing. My heart sank. Salamon was enraptured.

"Amazing!" He shaded his eyes against the raw sunlight. "Absolutely astonishing!"

"Old coot," Baksheesh said under his breath. "He'd find a skin rash fascinating."

Had I known where I was, had my head not been full of such questions as how we would stay alive, I would have agreed with Salamon. Yes, it was astonishing. The color, above all. It may have been a trick of the light, but the bare hills glowed as yellow-orange as a cantaloupe. Round openings pitted the whole flank of the farther slope like a honeycomb for a swarm of gigantic bees.

Shira stood, hands on hips, scanning the barren valley. Baksheesh sidled over to me.

"O Monarch of All You Survey," he said, "allow your devoted servant to inquire: Do you see a town? A village? A small hamlet, perhaps? This sun has blinded me; my eyes are full of grit. My vision is not as keen as usual. But you, Farsighted Eagle, surely you can observe a caravanserai? An oasis? A mud puddle?"

I told him to shut up. He kept on anyway.

"I am not a person of great learning. I must rack my brain for the precise word that expresses our situation eloquently. What would it be? Ah—something like: Lost."

I lied. I said I knew exactly where we were.

"So do I, Geographical Excellence," he said. "We are in the veritable center of the middle of nowhere."

"Did you ask the raïs for directions?" Shira broke in. "The innkeeper? Anybody?"

I said I didn't think I needed to.

I was afraid she would cloud up and rain all over me like those thunderstorms that occasionally batter Magenta. She only glanced at me with long-suffering annoyance. But there were no lightning bolts.

"Let me see the map," she said.

Until now, she had never asked and I had never offered. It hadn't seemed necessary. Baksheesh had poked his nose into all my belongings that day he made off with them. I was reluctant to show it to anyone else. Not that I mistrusted Shira. After all, I was in love with her. No, I simply kept it to myself.

We Magentans are brought up to be closemouthed about our business. Outside the family, we don't even like to admit what we ate for lunch.

I hiked up my shirt and fished out the parchment from its pouch at my waist. I carefully unfolded it and spread it on the ground.

Shira knelt and peered at it, tracing a finger from one edge to the other.

"This is what you found in the book?"

I nodded. "Yes. Just as I told you."

She studied it still more closely. She looked up at me.

"Kharr-loh," she said, "your map is wrong."

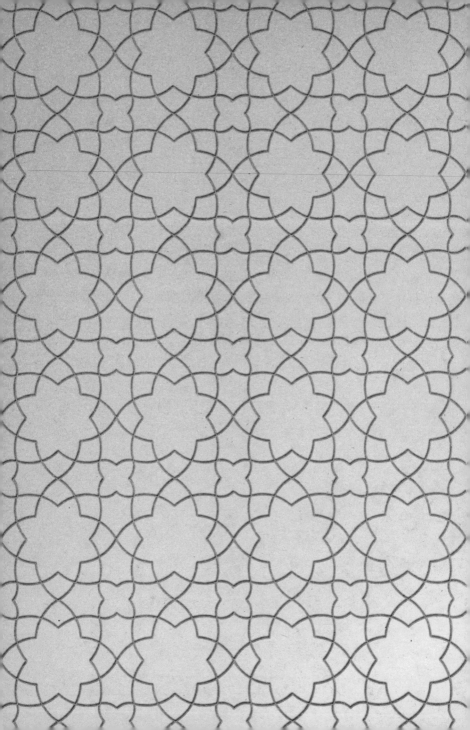

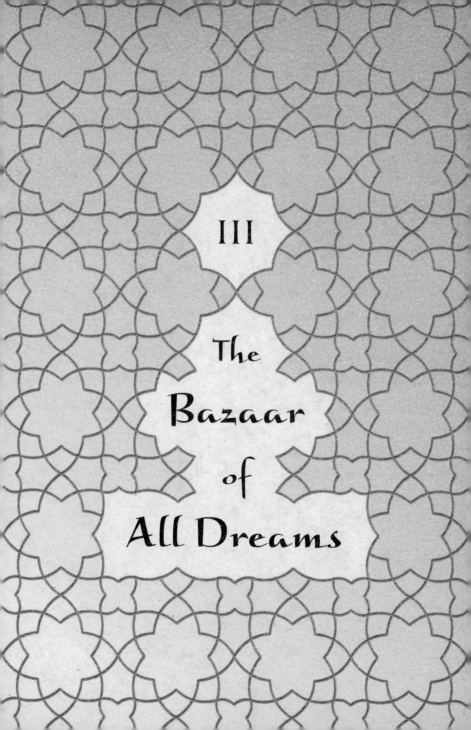

III

The Bazaar of All Dreams

19

I sat down fast. I had to, if I didn't want to fall in a heap. I tried not to be seasick in the middle of a desert. Not easy, for the ground kept opening beneath me and tilting back and forth. Uncle Evariste had been right from the start. The whole business was a fraud. And I, Carlo the Chooch, was stupid enough to be caught up in it.

"So," I said, when I stopped shaking and was able to say anything at all, "it's a forgery. Trash."

Shira shook her head. "No. Not exactly. It's old. Very old. I'm sure of that. I think it's real—for what it is. But—what is it?

"There's no sense in it," she went on. "It's half right—in some ways. Wrong in others. Things aren't where they're supposed to be. From what I can see, my caravanserai should be in a valley—here." She laid a finger on the map. "There's no valley. There should be a river nearby, but it's somewhere else. As if everything has shifted around. And here—whoever made the map tried to draw what looks like a fortress. I grew up in these parts and there's no fortress, let alone a royal treasury.

"Some places look right," she said. "Here—Marakand's where it ought to be. But the rest? No. I don't know what to make of it."

"I do," I said. "What I make of it—it's useless."

I picked up the map and climbed to my feet—as best I could, considering everything was falling to pieces around me. I would have ripped the thing to shreds then and there. I was angry enough to do it. Not that it would have done any good. Angry at what? At the map for being wrong? At Shira for telling me so? But being angry, at least, felt better than being seasick.

I turned the parchment back and forth. I remembered that night at home when I came close to tearing it up. And didn't. Because I believed it was real. Despite all, I suppose I still did. Who draws a map that's wrong on purpose? There must be a reasonable answer. In any case, I had no heart to destroy it. I folded the parchment and slipped it back into its pouch.

"We're going to Marakand," I said at last.

"O Clear Voice of Wisdom," said Baksheesh, who had been eavesdropping on every word. "As I recall suggesting to you, we never should have left there in the first place."

"You're coming with me," I told Shira in my firmest karwan-bushi tone, hoping to head off any objections she might come up with. She made no comments one way or the other, which made me a little uneasy. Baksheesh, however, had brightened. Until he heard the rest of what I had to say.

"We start all over again," I went on, as Baksheesh groaned. "This time, we'll do better."

If I hoped to find the treasure, I needed a more accurate map. Caravan masters would surely have one. Or merchants, or other travelers. Or, for that matter, the Thieves' Market.

"I said I'd see you home first," I added to Shira. "And so I will."

"But then, Most Resolute of Karwan-bushis," put in Baksheesh, resigned though not at all happy, "how shall we do this? It would be senseless, as you so shrewdly perceive, to wander through this boneyard of a desert. Especially—forgive me for calling this to Your Worthy Attention—since you have no idea where you are. And, Shining Lamp of Intelligence, if you have no idea where you are, it follows you have no idea where you're going."

"I do," I said. "The way we came. We'll retrace our steps."

"What?" blurted Baksheesh. "We turned off to keep clear of the fighting. The Kajiks—"

"Well, then, damn the Kajiks," I burst out. "And the Karakits. And the caravan robbers. To Jehannum with the lot! If we have to deal with them, we'll deal with them."

Some of this—most of it, all of it—was bravado and a good measure of sheer wind. Since I saw no other choice, I might as well put a bold face on it.

"To Jehannum?" Baksheesh retorted. "We'll soon be there ourselves. Before that, can we at least eat breakfast?"

So unsettled was I by Shira's opinion of the map, only then did I notice an obvious absence.

Salamon was missing.

I looked toward the animals. He was not with them. Nor anywhere else I could see.

I took Baksheesh by the arm. "Where is he? Where did he go?"

"How should I know?" Baksheesh shrugged. "He can't be far. No doubt the old buzzard spied an irresistibly charming fungus and had to make a note of it. Not that there's so much as a toadstool to be found here."

I should have kept a better eye on him. I went back a little way up the trail, calling out; then turned and started across the desert floor. I saw no one in either direction. Only echoes answered my shouts.

"Could he have gone in there?" Shira pointed to the honeycomb of chambers in the rocky slope.

Of course. How could he have resisted? Yes, and got himself into who knows what mischief. I told Baksheesh to bring the animals. With Shira leading her mare, we set off across a flat table of sand up to our ankles. At close range, the openings were bigger than I'd first calculated, stretching in a long row to form something like an arcade or open-fronted gallery. Shira had guessed right. Moments later, Salamon popped out from one of them, waving his arms, beckoning us to hurry.

I had prepared a few words to say to him about wandering off. I had no heart to reproach him, I was too relieved to find him safe; besides, he was beaming like the happiest child in the world.

"Come. Quickly!" he called. "Most remarkable. There's water—I found a pool deeper inside. I didn't venture much beyond. But—marvelous!"

The cavern was not as dark as I'd expected. Shafts of sunlight fell from circular holes higher up in the wall. I had no time to look around, for Salamon kept nudging us along a corridor of beaten earth. As he had said, in the middle of a high-domed grotto was a pool of clear water. I scooped up some in my cupped palm and cautiously tasted. It was fresh and ice cold.

I would have filled our water bags then and there, but Salamon pressed us to go farther. We left the animals to drink and followed him.

"Amazing!" he said. "I've never seen anything more astonishing."

"So, astonish me," Baksheesh retorted. "Amaze me with a ten-course feast laid out and waiting for us."

"Better than that," Salamon said. "Marvelous pictures."

"Pictures?" squawked Baksheesh. "I haven't had a night's sleep or a decent meal, I'm falling away to a shadow of my former self—and you're jabbering about pictures? In a cave? In the middle of a desert? Now I know for sure the sun has fried your wits."

The light dimmed as we made our way deeper into the cavern. On a smooth stretch of wall, a painting covered the surface with such brilliant colors that it glowed of itself.

It wasn't the style of picture I was used to. At first, I saw only a hodgepodge of flat shapes, one crowding against another. I looked closer and they suddenly came clear. As if the painter had viewed it from a hilltop overlooking a half-moon of bright blue water.

Ships were tied up at the docks. And, past the breakwater, a boat with a shredded sail—it reminded me of the leaky tub I practically rowed to Sidya. A jumble of buildings along the quayside. A marketplace—I swear I saw the bookstall where everything had begun.

The cold air must have given me chills. I was trembling all over and aching down to the marrow of my bones.

Shira stepped beside me. "What's wrong, Kharr-loh?"

"This can't be," I said. "But it is. See there? The Casa Galliardi. And there—my uncle's house. It's the port of Magenta."

Baksheesh had come to squint at the picture. "Extreme Worthiness, I very much doubt that. Like Saltimbocca here, you've had a touch of sun. One port's the same as another."

"No," I said. "I was born there. It's my home."

I heard footsteps scraping over the rough floor behind me. I swung around, reaching for my tulwar.

20

"Peace be upon you, friends."

A bandy-legged little man stood holding a torch in one hand. His beard was so spattered and stained I could not guess its original color. Knotted around his waist, a length of rope secured his trousers. Splotches of dried paint seemed the only things keeping his clothing from parting company.

"I thought I heard voices. I'm delighted that you came to visit."

"Not on purpose," grumbled Baksheesh.

"Even so," the man said, "I hope you have found something of interest."

"Remarkable," put in Salamon. "Absolutely fascinating."

"This is your work?" Shira said.

The little man bobbed his head. "Such as it is."

"Oh no," Baksheesh said aside to me. "A dauber! A paint-splasher! How did we come to fall in with one of them? Here, of all places? Rascals! Bad as public storytellers. Worse! They fling colors every which way and fool us into thinking they mean something. That's an honest living?"

"Honest as anything else in the world, and a living like another," said our host, whose ears must have been as sharp as his eyes.

"I am called Cheshim," he went on, taking no offense at Baksheesh's mumblings, smiling agreeably as I named each of us to him.

"And you," he said, turning his glance back to me—very cordially, as much at ease as if we had been old acquaintances. And for an instant I had half a notion we had met somewhere before. "This seems to have caught your attention. I take that as a compliment."

"The town, the harbor—" I said. "You've been to Magenta."

"Been to where?" Cheshim raised a paint-crusted eyebrow. "No, my young friend, I've not set foot beyond this place for—how many years? So many I hardly remember where I was before I came here."

"He's beginning to natter like old Salonica," Baksheesh said under his breath. "Two of a kind, if you ask me. One worse than the other. But which?"

"Mirza Cheshim, you may have forgotten," I said, "but surely you were there. You had to be. You saw the port. You painted it."

"I did?" Cheshim blinked. "Yes, yes, indeed so. If you believe you recognize it, I couldn't be better pleased. But, you see, I only paint whatever fancies float into my head. I haven't the least idea what's coming along, or when. How could I know what I'm doing until I've done it? In a manner of speaking, then, I really have nothing to do with them. They more or less decide for themselves, and always surprise me."

"But, mirza," Shira put in, "why do your work where no one sees it?"

"On the contrary," said Cheshim, "they are here for all who are meant to see them. And those who are meant to see them will unmistakably find them.

"I have others," he added. "You are welcome to look."

"Marvelous," said Salamon. "It would be a pleasure."

"I can hardly wait," said Baksheesh. "But, before I'm able to devote my full attention and admiration for—for whatever it is you do, I have to build up my strength. I suppose you must eat like everyone else—except for old Salami here," Baksheesh added. "Would you possibly have a little something in the way of food?"

"I have ample provisions," Cheshim replied. "I shall happily share them."

Baksheesh licked his lips and perked up. "I'm glad to hear that. I was afraid you wouldn't have much of a larder in this barren nowhere."

"The birds bring everything I need," Cheshim said. "Eagles, hawks, ravens—they fly over quite often. I gather what they drop."

"You eat bird droppings?" Baksheesh eyed him queasily. "Not to disrespect your hospitality, but never mind about offering refreshments."

"No, no," Cheshim corrected. "They leave off tidbits, odds and ends of all sorts. Only the other day, a seagull passed by—"

"Astonishing," put in Salamon. "So far inland—wherever this part of inland may be? I definitely must make a note of that."

"Yes, and left a very tasty fish head," Cheshim went on. "Not long ago, a charming little bulbul flew by. Too small to carry much, but he perched up in the rocks and sang sweetly all night. That was better than a meal."

"In other words," Baksheesh said, "the pickings here are rather slim." He shrugged. "Eh, well, I suppose something is better than nothing. The fish head—I'm not so sure about that."

"And your marvelous colors, mirza?" Salamon asked, as Cheshim led us farther down the passageway. "Where do you manage to find them?"

"Here," Cheshim said, lighting lamps set in niches along the wall. "Dig deep enough, you're likely to turn up anything you want. Raw pigments I grind for my paints. Brushes?" He chuckled and pointed a gnarled finger at his beard. "Those, I grow myself."

My shock at seeing Magenta had begun draining away. I had pretty much decided Baksheesh was right. One port was like another. My imagination had misled me.

But, if I had been taken aback, now it was Shira's turn. I heard her draw in her breath. She went closer to the next picture. From what I could see, it simply showed a wide river lined with willow trees. Snow-covered mountains dwarfed the rest of the scene.

"We call those mountains the 'Roof of the World,'" she murmured. "That river is near my inn. The last crossing before the borders of Cathai. I know the spot.

"My brother and I played there. Yes, exactly—there. We called it 'our' river. We made believe it belonged to us and no one else.

"See the long slope to the water's edge?" Shira said. "That's where my father taught me to swim. I loved that spot. Sometimes I would go to sit there by myself, always wondering what was on the far shore and beyond. There was a bridge a little way downstream, but I was afraid to cross it.

"When I grew older, I was too busy with my work. I still dreamed of reaching the other side; but I went there no longer."

She turned from the picture. Her eyes shone with tears.

I said I had never seen her cry.

"Nor will you again."

Salamon was urging us to see more of Cheshim's pictures. I was sorry I did.

The next painting showed a caravan under attack, camels butchered, fallen to their knees, horsemen galloping on shaggy ponies. In an upper corner of the picture were the faces of dead men, eye sockets empty, mouths gaping; patches of flesh had rotted away to show the white glint of skulls.

Cheshim stood waiting behind me.

"Mirza," I said, "do you paint your nightmares?"

"Not mine." He gave me a slantwise look. "Yours, perhaps?"

"You told me you painted whatever fancies came into your head," I began. "But you show things that have really happened."

"If you say so." He shrugged. "I have no idea if they ever happened, or will happen. Or may never happen at all. And some I have had to leave unfinished."

Shira and Salamon had gone on ahead, with Baksheesh grumbling to himself and anyone who cared to listen. I went quickly to catch up with them.

Other pictures covered the wall. I gave them not much more than a glance. I did understand what Cheshim meant when he claimed to paint his dreams. Like so many dreams—certainly my own—they had a good many odd bits and pieces; and he had put them all together in one picture. They confused and unsettled me. I had seen enough of them. And, by now, I was starting to agree with Baksheesh. I would have welcomed a little something to put in my stomach, even if it was what the birds had left.

I found Shira in front of one of the larger pictures; and, to me, the most perplexing. She had put her hand to her mouth and was staring wide-eyed. Cheshim had depicted what appeared to be a fortress under siege. Warriors had breached the walls and streamed into an open square, putting men, women, and children to the sword. At one side, within a chamber, a man in royal robes flung jewels and golden objects into a deep pit.

"I know what this is," she said. "But not as it's shown here. Not with—him."

I followed her gaze. In the upper portion of the scene, against a crimson sky, a towering figure dominated the slaughter below. In an upraised hand, he held a blazing globe.

I could not read the expression on Shira's face. It may have been part fury, part fear.

She said one word.

"Charkosh."

21

She swung around to confront Cheshim, who had been watching her closely.

"You know this man?" she said, more an accusation than a question. "You've seen him. He was here—"

"No, dushizéh." Cheshim spread his hands. "I assure you he was not. Seen him? Only in a manner of speaking. As the picture came to mind."

I put a hand on her shoulder. "These are his dreams. Not yours, not mine. We see what we want to see."

I meant to calm her. I didn't believe a word of what I was saying.

"Those are his dreams?" Baksheesh put in. "How does he sleep at night? I can tell you all his daubs and spatters have taken away my appetite."

"Forgive me, mirza," Cheshim said. "That was not my intention."

"What was your intention, then?" I asked.

Cheshim smiled. "What was yours?"

"I had none," I said. "You were the one who showed us these things."

"I offered. You looked," Cheshim said pleasantly. "You saw what you saw."

"I warned you against these paint-daubers," Baksheesh whispered. "Admirable Excellence, they do nothing but confuse the brain."

In this the hermit-artist had amply succeeded. At least, I had a glimpse of the man Shira would have gone after with a carving knife. Assuming it was a good likeness, the face was as cruel as any I had ever seen.

Salamon turned to Shira. "Did I hear you say you found the scene familiar?"

"Yes." Shira had command of herself again. "It makes me think of a story my mother told when my brother and I were children. The tale of Tarik Beg and the Dark Fortress.

"As the legend goes, in days long gone by, Tarik Beg was the sar, the ruler of the Kashgari folk. Word came to him that the tribe of Hunzuks were on the move, and would, before many days, attack him and his people.

"Terror struck the hearts of the Kashgaris, for the Hunzuk hordes were known as ruthless pillagers and looters; worse than a swarm of locusts. It was said that where a Hunzuk set foot, grass never grew again.

"The Kashgaris first thought to flee their town and take with them what valuables they could carry. But Tarik Beg urged against this. 'The Hunzuks will only track you down and strip you of all you own,' he told them. 'Better you should hide your family treasures out of their reach. When they find nothing worth the taking, they will go their way and seek riches elsewhere.

"'I give you leave to bring your most valued possessions to my stronghold. I will store them for safekeeping in my own treasure chamber. My fortress can withstand any attack. Thus, when the danger is past, you will come and claim what is yours.'

"The Kashgaris were grateful for the kindness and generosity of Tarik Beg, who then commanded a shaft to be dug in the middle of the treasure chamber, with tunnels and side passages far underground. To assure them further, he declared that he would likewise hide all his treasure along with theirs.

"The Kashgaris toiled day and night, night and day, and the work was soon completed. Tarik Beg was the first to store his treasures in the farthest reaches of the tunnels. The Kashgaris then bore their possessions to safety. The wealthiest of the merchants brought heirlooms of great worth; the poorest folk carried in their humble belongings, which they prized nonetheless. It surprised Tarik Beg to see such a quantity of goods.

"'How do they come to have so much of value?' he said to himself. 'Are they more prosperous than I thought? Or have they not paid sufficient tribute to me?'

"When all had been concealed, the mouth of the shaft was covered over with tiles from the chamber floor, so carefully and cleverly it could not be seen that anything lay below.

"As feared, the day came when Hunzuk pillagers swarmed into the town. What befell the Kashgaris was not what Tarik Beg had foretold.

"True, his fortress stood fast, the Hunzuks could not breach it. However, finding no booty in the town only enraged them. Instead of going their way, the furious Hunzuks set fire to every house, then turned their vengeance on the townsfolk.

"The Kashgaris fled to the fortress, pleading to be let in so they could take refuge there. But Tarik Beg turned a deaf ear to their entreaties.

"'They are too many,' he said to himself. 'Do they expect me to save them all? Am I to pick and choose? That would be unfair. Worse, if I open my doors, the Hunzuks will follow after them and overrun my fortress. Thus, we would all perish.'

"And so, he did not unbar his doors. Many were slain even as they cried for mercy at his gates. When the marauding Hunzuks grew arm-weary and sated with bloodshed, they rode off empty-handed.

"The folk who lived through the slaughter gathered again

at the fortress. They angrily reproached Tarik Beg and railed against him for leaving them to a bloody fate. They clamored for the return of their treasures brought to him for safe-keeping.

"Again, Tarik Beg would hear none of their demands. 'This cannot be done,' he declared. 'It is impossible now for all the goods to be sorted out. Some may even be mixed with my own. How shall the rightful owners be known when many of them are slain? The others may try to profit and claim what is not truly theirs.

"'That would be a gross injustice and I will have no hand in it,' he said. 'Therefore, it is only fitting and proper that I keep it all. Had I not stored it here, the Hunzuks would have taken it and it would have been lost in any case. Besides, I am the sar. Who dares to gainsay me?'

"The townsfolk, outraged, spoke among themselves:

"'As this treacherous sar would not let us in,' they said to one another, 'we will not let him out.'

"And so they barred, bolted, and sealed up every means of leaving the fortress. Not so much as a beetle could escape from it. The story goes that Tarik Beg died mad in his own treasure chamber. The Kashgaris left the wreckage of their town and made new lives for themselves elsewhere."

This was hardly the most cheerful story I had ever heard. I was half sorry Shira had told it. At the same time, it made me think of my map. I had to admit it was wrong, as she had shown it to be. And yet there was a spot marked as a royal treasury. What to make of that? I had a moment of hope, but it flickered out as she went on.

"None can be sure if it is true, or only a tale that mothers weave to teach their children to keep their word. The Dark Fortress is long gone. Wind and weather have had their way with it; the earth swallowed it up and buried it—if it ever existed to begin with. Even if it did, who knows where it once stood?"

"I do," said Baksheesh.

Another glimmer of hope winked out faster than the first when he added: "All over the place. Anywhere. Everywhere. I know these Keshavaris. They keep dreaming of what once was a grand empire. Why they waste their time on it, that's beyond me."

"Beyond me, as well," put in Salamon. "An empire? Rather like keeping an elephant, I should say. An impressive creature, I grant you. But—the effort and expense of tending it? Who would want one?"

"I'm telling you," Baksheesh said, "if there's so much as a bump in the road, they'll claim it used to be a palace, a castle, the remains of a glorious city—why, they'll swear their local horse trough's built on top of some old king's pleasure garden; and charge you to admire it.

"You want a fortress? A royal treasury? Seek on, O Paragon

of Perseverance. You'll find dozens. Long buried, of course, so you won't see them. At least, you can say you found them and go home in triumph."

Cheshim then invited us to visit his workroom, promising refreshments afterward. I had no stomach for bird-dropped delicacies. Pictures—I had seen more than I wanted. They unsettled, even frightened me; and, despite his good nature, so did Cheshim.

As the others followed him farther into the cavern, I took Shira's arm. I had something I wanted to say without everyone horning in.

"I've been wondering for a while—now more than ever," I began, hesitating but finding no better way to put it.

"Am I a fool to keep looking for something that isn't there? With a map that leads nowhere?"

"That," she said, "would be your decision."

"Cheshim showed me my home," I said. "I was glad to leave, but I miss it. Even so—am I foolish if I never go home at all?"

"Stay in Keshavar? Why?"

I shuffled around and finally said, "Well—for you."

She hesitated only a long moment. To me, it felt like hours.

"No," she said at last. "You are a ferenghi. It would not suit you."

Her mother, I reminded her, had wed a ferenghi.

"They loved each other," she said.

"Yes," I said. "So I thought it might be—You. And I—" I was getting knots in my tongue and had to leave off. I was sure she understood exactly what I meant.

She shook her head. "Kharr-loh," she said in a voice I scarcely heard, "Kharr-loh, if I could love anyone, it would be you."

22

I wanted to explore Shira's remark a little further; but here came Salamon, bright-faced from his glimpse of Cheshim's workplace.

"Most remarkable how he's set himself up," Salamon told us, while the hermit-artist led us back through the passageways into open air and sunlight. "He's found stones to make mortars and pestles to grind his pigments. He mixes the most astonishing colors. You really should see for yourself."

I said I'd be glad to. Next time I was in the neighborhood.

"Don't bother. The place is a caravanserai for bats," Baksheesh said to me. "I hate to think what else lives there."

"Mirza Cheshim," Salamon said, "you were telling us of your next picture. Altogether fascinating."

"Ah, so I was, so I was," Cheshim said. "Alas, I have had to leave it unfinished.

"What came to me one night—how shall I put it?—yes, it was a kind of tale. A well-digger loved a princess but never dared to tell her, for he was too poor. Then he found a bottle belonging to a genie and wouldn't return it until the genie granted him vast riches—the foolish well-digger thought wealth would win her heart. He disguised himself as a great prince and brought her chests of treasures."

Baksheesh gave me a look. "I've heard that tune before."

"But the princess refused him," Cheshim went on, "because her heart was secretly given to a humble well-digger. So, he wished for all his fortune to vanish and went back to her as the poor well-digger that he was."

Cheshim paused. "Ah, forgive me. I have neglected your refreshments."

"I can hardly wait," said Baksheesh.

As the hermit-artist hurried away, I turned to Salamon. It surprised me, I told him, that Cheshim was willing to talk of his unfinished work to strangers.

"On the contrary," Salamon said. "These fellows are pathetically eager to tell anyone willing to listen. In fact, once they start, and have the bit in their teeth, it's next to impossible to make them leave off."

"I'll tell you something else," Baksheesh retorted. "He claims he dreamed all that? No. He's a faker. A liar. It's the same tale that wretch of a storyteller was spouting in Marakand."

Baksheesh was right. I, too, recognized it. As for wishing away a fortune, I had practically offered to do likewise with Shira only minutes ago.

"Yes, I recall it, too," Salamon agreed. "I should guess it's an old, familiar story. Cheshim no doubt heard it as a child. It stuck in his memory and his dreams."

"Well and good, as far as it goes," Baksheesh said. "Except for the end. That pestilential ragbag stopped short. He didn't tell the best part. I did. I made it up off the top of my head as we walked along."

Shira nodded. "True."

"So he's not only a faker and a liar," Baksheesh indignantly declared. "He's a thief. I don't know how, but he stole it from me. Paint-dauber? He's a mind-robber."

Baksheesh scowled and snapped his mouth shut as Cheshim reappeared. The artist carried an armful of flat, polished stones that served as plates for whatever it was he had piled on them. He motioned for us to sit on the beaten earth of a kind of portico that shaded us from the sun. Not to insult him, I made a show of dipping into my portion, which turned out to be surprisingly tasty. In fact, I wolfed it down.

"I must thank you for doing me a service." Cheshim beamed at Shira, then at me. "My unfinished picture—the dream faded. The faces of the princess and the well-digger escaped me. I was unable to continue.

"Now that I see you two young people, their features are clear to me again. They are yours. You have allowed me to finish my painting. I am ever grateful. You are welcome to stay and see my work completed. It should take no more than six or seven months."

Salamon, I was sure, would have been overjoyed to spend half a year in the cave; but I thanked Cheshim for his kind invitation. Time pressed, we had to be on our way.

"Young men are always in a hurry," Cheshim said. "Without prying into your business, may I ask what way that is? Perhaps I can help you."

He seemed eager to be useful, and so I explained how we had come from Marakand and now planned to retrace our steps there. We needed new gear; and, I mentioned in passing, I hoped to find a better map. Of the treasure, of course, I said nothing.

"No need for many weeks of travel," Cheshim said. "There is a town much closer. What's it called? I misremember. Something like Shahryar—ah, yes, Shahryar-eh-Ghermezi. I passed through it on my way here. When? I don't recall. It must have been a good while ago. You will surely find everything you require. Not a comfortable journey; but, in the long run, to your best advantage."

I certainly had no heart to turn back; nor did I relish spending several miserable weeks only to end where we started. I had no misgivings—until Cheshim went on.

"It's very simple," he said. "Follow the desert straight ahead until you run out of food. Then, turn right. Keep on your way until you run out of water. The town will be practically in front of you. Really, you can't miss it."

Easy enough directions. All we had to do was pay attention and notice when we were starving and dying of thirst, conditions hard to ignore.

I glanced at Shira, who gave a brief nod. Salamon, I was sure, would have walked happily to the moon and found it extremely interesting. Baksheesh looked sour, but he would have looked sour in any case.

I got to my feet and stared at the pink sand and the cantaloupe-colored hills with their jagged outcroppings. Yes, Salamon's constant wonderment must have rubbed off a little on me, for I found them astonishingly beautiful.

And I hated them. They could kill us all.

What a real karwan-bushi, with all his wits about him, would have decided—I had no idea. I did the only sensible thing.

"We'll try it," I said.

23

Sharing some grand purpose can forge unbreakable bonds of comradeship. So can boredom.

Of that, we had enough to go around, with plenty left over: the everyday messiness; yawning grumpiness in the morning; afternoon annoyances; weariness at nightfall; and the same to do all over again at daybreak.

As for foul odors, they came in a variety I had never imagined. We surely smelled as bad as the camels. Maybe worse. Luckily, we got used to it and stopped noticing. Also, we kept busy hawking sand out of our lungs. Even Shira, to the extent that such a thing was possible, looked haggard and drawn.

Salamon, of course, was good tempered as ever, always in the best of spirits—which vexed Baksheesh more than anything else.

"Disgusting old codger," he grumbled. "Why can't he be miserable like the rest of us? I ask you, O Noblest Karwan-bushi, where's justice in the world?"

We had, by then, decided to walk our animals. It would have been too heartless to burden the camels by riding them. Shira and her mare plodded along through sand above our ankles. Baksheesh, bringing up the rear, turned into more of a camel-pusher than a camel-puller. I trudged beside Salamon and the donkey, who had grown all the more devoted to him.

I remarked, a little sourly, that if he meant to reach the sea, he had chosen a dry way of finding it.

"Not at all," he said, with his smile of happy innocence. "I am completely confident I shall arrive sooner or later. It is a simple matter of pressing on.

"So, by all logic, you are bound to end up wherever you wish. Though it may not always be where you think it is. In any case, getting there is as interesting as being there."

The sea, that day, was less on his mind than Cheshim's pictures. They troubled me, as well; I would have been glad to forget them. Salamon must have been pondering them since leaving the artist's cave.

"My brain isn't as nimble as it used to be," he said. "Cheshim showed a scene from the old tale of Tarik Beg— but what was Charkosh doing there? He doesn't belong in the picture, and yet Cheshim painted him."

I had my own questions. Since I found no answers, I had to set them aside. I told Salamon they were only fancies that meant nothing.

"All dreams are true, if you know how to look at them," Salamon said. "What they tell us we don't always understand. We need to put the bits and pieces together. The ball of fire that Charkosh was holding—it made me think of the Kajiks and Karakits burning down the village. And what did the innkeeper say about it? Flames no one could put out?

"It reminds me of something called 'Greek Fire.' Once lit, it was unquenchable," he went on. "In ancient times, people in your part of the world used it against their enemies. Fortunately, they gave it up. They may have found it too horrible. Or, most likely, they forgot how to make it.

"I had a classmate at the university, more years ago than I can count. He had the foolish notion of discovering the lost recipe and making his fortune from it. By then, no one was sure if it had really existed or was only old folklore. But he kept at it, cooking up every ingredient he could think of.

"We urged him on—we were as foolish as he was—and so he boiled, and mashed, and simmered, toiling away over his beakers, distillation coils, and retorts. What he ended up with was a bucket of the most vile-smelling concoction that turned your stomach and brought tears to your eyes.

"He gave up after that. But the question arose: What to do with the substance? We couldn't keep it, but how to get rid of the mess?

"I must confess, my boy," Salamon added, "the dean of our faculty and I had always been at loggerheads. He considered me a natural-born troublemaker; and I considered him a great bag of wind. I suggested pouring the stuff down his chimney and into his bedchamber.

"What pranksters we were in those days. In the middle of the night, we all climbed to the roof, found the flue that went to his fireplace, tipped up the bucket, and sent the awful mess flooding down.

"Before we could clamber from the rooftop, the dean burst out of his chamber, still in his nightshirt, coughing, gasping, holding his nose, babbling that some evil fiend had tried to poison him in his sleep.

"Nightcap askew, he bumbled into the street, gulping fresh air. Alas, he saw us on the rooftop and understood we were the evil fiends. He shook his fist, raved and ranted all the more since the vile odor had wafted through the lecture halls, refectories, and dormitories. The street was aboil with professors, tutors, and distinguished scholars scrambling to flee the stench.

"He ordered the provost to give us a most magisterial thrashing. My fellow students were heavily fined. To me, he granted a special favor, for which I have been ever grateful.

"He expelled me," said Salamon. "I could not have been better pleased. It allowed me to attend the best of all schools."

"And that was . . . ?" I asked.

"The world, my boy," he said. "The most rigorous of academies, but the curriculum is excellent. For a time, I conducted classes free of charge, and taught in market squares, taverns, innyards—until I realized my students knew more than I did.

"And so I set off on my own road wherever it led me." Salamon blinked and shook his head. "But now, my lad, I fear I've lost my train of thought. It will come back to me. I shall puzzle it out. You can think your way through a brick wall if you keep at it."

Following Salamon's mental processes was like strolling down a garden path with unexpected twists and turns and odd things popping out from the hedges. What he had in mind I could not imagine, let alone picture him as having been a troublemaker and prankster.

He was still pondering when we halted for the last meal of the day—an occasion I had come to dread. Our food was so disheartening I looked forward to going hungry.

Cheshim had given us all he could spare. Very good it was, for whatever it was; but not enough to last us any length of time. We had to fall back on the reserves of our own provisions.

These had gained a life of their own in the form of weevils and other tiny creatures not even Salamon was able to identify.

At first, we pried them loose at knifepoint, but they out-numbered their host; and, finally, we ate them as part of the menu.

At least they were fresh. I preferred them to the scrapings from the bottom of our sacks: what looked like pieces of old rope dipped in tar. I suppose they nourished us; but they were an acquired taste, and one I never acquired. Given the oppor-tunity, I would have been tempted to trade both camels and Baksheesh himself for a few links of good Magenta sausage. I envied Salamon's lack of appetite.

I expected us to be roasted by day and frozen when the sun went down. I had not reckoned on the wind. The bare crags on either side of us funneled unceasing currents that swirled and fishtailed around us and crept into our tents when we tried to sleep.

Mostly it blew straight into our faces. As did the sand. Every grain stung like a hornet. The camels clamped their nostrils shut. We draped rags over the noses of the mare and donkey, and did likewise for ourselves. The sand still filtered through the fabric. It invaded our clothing, scraped and chafed, and it was no use trying to dust it off or shake it loose.

Starvation can sour anyone's disposition. Not that we were at one another's throats, but certainly on one another's nerves.

And I had my own bedevilments. My decision had put us all at risk, but my thoughts above all were for Shira. I could blame only myself and my search for the treasure in the first place. When Shira had told me she was leaving—if I truly loved her, I should have let her go. Even insisted on it. Wherever else, at least she wouldn't be in this nightmare of a desert.

What had Salamon said when the bandits had been so brutally killed, and I had a hand in it? Only one thing you can't do, nor can anyone. Undo what you've done. It hadn't comforted me then. It didn't comfort me now.

Astonishingly, Cheshim's reckoning proved exact. After our last breakfast, we saw a trail opening to our right. It was rock-strewn, more gravel than sand. We followed it. The wind didn't pursue us.

Salamon assured us we were well on our way to Shahryar-eh-Ghermezi. "Very simple and logical," he said. "Cheshim told us to keep straight until we ran out of water. As we have very little of it left, logically we should be there reasonably soon. Perhaps within a few days. And just as well, since no one can go without water much longer than that."

"No one but you," Baksheesh retorted. "You're already dry as a stick of kindling. A parched pomegranate! A shriveled-up old fig! That paint-dauber claimed we'd be at Shahryar-eh-whatever when our water ran out? What if we poured it all into the ground right now? Then it would be right here in front of us. You want logic? There's logic for you."

"Well reasoned, my camel-pulling friend," said Salamon,

taking this outburst in stride. "But logic often has nothing to do with reality."

Cheshim had, so far, been accurate. What if his calculations, this time, were off by only a couple of days? I judged it wiser not to take the risk. And so we hoarded every drop of water, giving more to our animals than to ourselves.

I don't know if it was hunger or thirst that turned me light-headed. By the end of our second day, my lips had cracked open, my throat felt as if a salted codfish had been stuffed down it. I could not so much as spit; not that I had a mind to do so. Thirst, I saw, was taking its toll on Shira, but she made sure the mare drank her fill.

Baksheesh suffered more than any of us. Instead of walking, he lurched. Instead of him pulling the camels, the camels were pulling him. The ground, at least, had grown softer, almost spongy. We were grateful for that. But if there was a stone anywhere along our path, Baksheesh was sure to trip over it.

Next day, he vanished from the face of the earth.

24

Among the odds and ends I learned from the raïs during that nightmare caravan, one was: Stragglers were doomed. Travelers at the rear of the column, without realizing it, tended to lag behind. Little by little, the gap between them and the main body widened. The camels, when roped head to tail, plodded steadily forward; but the journeyers on foot, or on horseback, had to move faster and faster. In no time, the caravan could outdistance them. By then, it was too late. There was no way they could catch up. Separated, isolated from the group, for all practical purposes they were lost.

So I always kept an eye on Baksheesh. Salamon trudged as usual beside the donkey; Shira, with her mare. Baksheesh had stopped having anything to do with the pack animals. And I, as well as being the karwan-bushi, took up the profession of camel-puller.

Last time I had glanced back at him, Baksheesh was managing well enough on his own, limping along the soft shoulder of the trail. Now I turned and saw him sitting on the ground. Or so it seemed. First, I thought he had stopped to console his bunions. I was about to tell him to get a move on. Until I realized the lower half of him had disappeared.

At that moment, with Shira at his heels, Salamon went running past me. Baksheesh, meanwhile, was yelling at the top of his voice, waving his arms, and gradually sinking from view.

By the time I reached him, his shoulders already had vanished; his arms waved frantically in the air but they, too, looked about to submerge.

Salamon motioned me to keep away. He had taken the donkey's rope halter and now trod cautiously, testing the ground at every step. Baksheesh puffed and snorted. Salamon tossed the rope at him.

"Take hold," he called. "Stop flapping about; it will only make matters worse. And keep your mouth shut," he added, for Baksheesh was spitting out gobs of what seemed to be a syrupy mess of wet dirt.

"Quicksand," Shira said between her teeth. "Idiot. How did he get himself into it?"

If quicksand could be found anywhere in Keshavar, Baksheesh would be sure to step in it. I had heard only vaguely of quicksand: a harmless-looking patch of earth that would swallow an unwary traveler in the blink of an eye.

This is not altogether true. As I later learned from Salamon, drowning in quicksand takes a long time; in fact it's close to impossible unless you set your mind on it.

The real danger, in this case, was that Baksheesh, like all of us, was exhausted and not much able to follow Salamon's instructions. On top of that, the two of them were at cross purposes.

The more Salamon urged him to stay calm, the more the frantic Baksheesh flung himself about. He kept sinking deeper, then bobbing up again, snorting and choking. He did have enough of his wits left to seize the end of the rope and hang on to it.

"Excellent," Salamon reassured him. "Now, lie back as if you were floating in a bathtub."

"I should know bathtubs?" muttered Baksheesh between mouthfuls of sand.

He did, at last, float to the surface. Shira and I helped Salamon haul on the rope and dragged him clear. By this time, Baksheesh was so thoroughly soaked and covered with brownish wet sand that he looked like a loaf of gingerbread. Once on solid ground, he dropped in a heap, head between his hands. As soon as he got his breath back and regained some of his strength, he wailed as much as he had done while we were heaving him out.

"Accursed pit!" he blubbered. "Every evil imp in Keshavar had me by the heels. I was at the gates of Jehannum!"

"Oh, I very much doubt that," Salamon said, by way of soothing him. "There's more Jehannum here aboveground than below it."

"That's what you think," Baksheesh retorted. "Then, old Spaghettini, answer me this: How did I come close to drowning in the middle of a desert?"

"There's water all around us. Sometimes a little of it seeps up to the surface," explained Salamon. "But there are great rivers and tributaries flowing beneath your feet. Like the veins and arteries under your skin."

"Under yours, not mine," Baksheesh said. "I know when I've been to Jehannum and back."

"Ungrateful wretch," I said, as Shira and I got him to his feet. "He saved your life and you don't give him so much as a word of thanks?"

"None required," put in Salamon. "Sooner or later he would have crawled out on his own."

"Aha!" cried Baksheesh. "There you hear him. He says so himself. Thank him? I won't. He insulted me when he called me softhearted. If anything, he owes me an apology."

I would have taken Baksheesh by the scruff of his neck and shaken a little gratitude out of him; but I was too thirsty to worry about polite behavior. So I let it pass.

Apart from having been terrified out of his wits, and

covered with mud rapidly drying on him like a brown shell, Baksheesh was none the worse for wear.

On the contrary: He talked about little else. His horrifying experience crowded out all his previous complaints. He even forgot about his bunions. Each time we halted, he trotted out some new detail he had neglected to mention. The pit, in his recollection, grew deeper and deeper, his struggles all the greater.

"I can tell you I never thought I'd see the light of day again," he declared, for the fifth or sixth time. "I was stifling, suffocating, my lungs bursting while the dreadful mess closed around me.

"How did I find the strength to free myself?" he blathered on. "Only the thought that you, O Noble Benefactor, would be lost without my services, leaving you in hopeless confusion. That gave me new heart as, inch by inch, I fought my way to the surface."

One thing had slipped his mind: Salamon, Shira, and I did not figure in his account. We might as well have not been there at all. I would have reminded him and taken him to task for it, but Shira motioned for me to let him ramble on.

Which he did. On the one hand, it passed the time and took our minds off our thirst. On the other—for an occasional fleeting moment and not in any serious way—I came close to wishing we had left him to fend for himself in the quicksand.

I blame those less-than-kindly thoughts on my own

difficulties. Water flowed through my waking moments—and sleeping ones, such as they were. I had never imagined it in so many enticing forms. Rivers, cascades, bubbling brooks, the public fountain in Magenta. Water in brimming glassfuls, in rain barrels, pitchers, buckets, all of it clear and sparkling.

Once, I dreamed I had finally discovered the royal treasury and found its endless chambers crammed with enormous jars of—water.

In reality, what was left at the bottom of our water bags stank. We drank it anyway.

Midmorning of the next day, I saw the town.

I gave a glad cry, which came out sounding like a duck in distress. I dropped the camel's rope and ran toward it. Shira put out a hand to hold me back. I pulled away and stumbled forward.

Shahryar-eh-Ghermezi was a sight to behold, more glorious than Cheshim had suggested. I stared breathless at sun-gilded towers, terraces of flowers, palm trees gently swaying in the breeze.

I noticed one unusual thing.

The town was floating in midair.

25

My legs decided I needed to fall down. By the time Shira reached me, my head was going in circles. Hanging just above the peaks, the town had begun receding into the distance.

I urged all haste. Before it sailed out of reach, we had to find ladders and a lot of rope. I thought I was being sensible and practical. I was probably babbling.

Shira laid a tender hand on my cheek. Such bliss! I wondered if I could arrange to fall down again.

"Kharr-loh, it is nothing," she said. "Only a tasvir."

Salamon came to kneel beside her. "What you see, my lad, is not what you think you see."

I stared around. "Have I gone mad?"

"No more than to be expected," he said. "The folk in your part of the world call it 'Fata Morgana.' A mirage, an illusion."

"I saw it," I insisted. "I still see it."

"As do we all," he said. "Yes, an excellent mirage. Very convincing. The golden towers are especially fine, I must make a note of that. But it is no more than the reflection of a town somewhere else, far away. As often as not, the mirage will be an oasis or watering place. A welcome sight. But travelers have lost their lives trying to reach it.

"There—yet not there," he added. "A trick of the light, the currents of air, and rays of the sun—"

"Pay no mind to that bag of bones," Baksheesh muttered to me. "He had the gall to tell me I had fallen into a mud puddle when I know I plunged into the bowels of the earth."

Baksheesh shaded his eyes. "I see what I see. That paint-dauber made fools of us. A town, yes. Did he mention it would be in the middle of the air?"

"It isn't." Shira had gotten to her feet. "You're looking in the wrong direction."

She pointed a little farther down the trail. I feared that she, too, had been caught up in an illusion. But, less than a quarter of a league away, unmistakably solid, rose the walls of Shahryar-eh-Ghermezi.

Cheshim once more proved to be correct. When my head cleared and I pulled myself together, we set off again. By the time we reached the gates, we had squeezed the last drops from the water bags.

The town had saved our lives, but I was a shade disappointed. Shahryar-eh-Ghermezi turned out to be far less imposing than the mirage. It struck me as a pleasant little market town not much bigger than its name. Cheshim had called it charming. I suppose it was. At the moment, it made no difference to me. All I wanted was to see our animals tended, to eat, drink, and sleep for a few months, preferably at the same time.

As far as that went, the town did have an advantage over the mirage. It was real. The streets bustled with water sellers and food vendors. We would have flung ourselves on them, bought out their whole stock, and looked around for more. But Salamon warned us to be cautious, to eat and drink sparingly at first. So we controlled our hunger as best we could. Except for Baksheesh. He waved away Salamon's advice, drank up most of the contents of a water seller's urn, stuffed himself with kebabs, pastries, and anything else he could fit into his mouth. He lost all of it soon after.

We did, without difficulty, find a small khan with well-kept stables and more or less clean rooms. I slept for what seemed a year or so but turned out to be a day and a half. I dimly recall taking a steam bath in the hammam, as did Shira and Salamon. If Baksheesh employed that facility, I couldn't tell the difference.

Restored to something close to human, I turned my attention to the reason we had come here in the first place. I wanted a better map.

At home, I had heard seafarers talk of what they called a "rutter." I understood it to be more than simply a chart; rather, a book giving details on coastlines, landmarks, shoals, and everything dealing with navigation. I wondered if there might be something like it for the Road of Golden Dreams. Also, in the port of Magenta, ship chandlers made a business of outfitting vessels with everything needed for a voyage. If such a place existed for caravans and overland travelers, it would spare us from having to provision ourselves piecemeal.

Cheshim had told us we could find everything we wanted in Shahryar-eh-Ghermezi. I took him at his word and we set out to look for this kind of establishment.

The bazaars here were small compared with those in Marakand. Instead of arranged according to trade and craft—for example, goldsmiths all in one street, rug merchants in another—shops of every kind jammed together higgledy-piggledy. It took some time before we found what I was searching for.

In the shop, so many saddles, bridles, coils of rope, water bags, and all manner of oddments filled the shelves and covered the floor that there was hardly room for the proprietor.

He popped up from behind a heap of blankets. Long-jawed, with the bushiest eyebrows I had ever seen, he welcomed us and introduced himself as Daftan. He assured us he could supply all provisions and equipment we wanted, and deliver them to our khan the next day.

I explained about the rutter and asked if I might buy one from him.

"What you seek is a 'ketab,' as we call it." He raised his thicket of eyebrows. "Yes, mirza, I understand exactly. Also you may wish to purchase a few phoenix tailfeathers? The recipe for Greek Fire? A sack of powdered unicorn horn?"

It took me a moment to realize he was joking at my expense. He went on: "Why stop there? Ask to buy my right arm. Or sell you my wife and children." Daftan snorted a laugh. He rolled up his eyes and addressed the ceiling. "Preserve me! Here comes a young ferenghi demanding a ketab as if ordering a leg of mutton."

I told him I got the point: He had none for sale.

"Never did, never expect to," he said. "If I did, would I sell it to you? No, mirza, ahead of you would be a line of the richest merchant travelers in Keshavar bidding against one another. You have no idea how rare and priceless it is. Had I such a thing, I would retire from trade, sit in the shade, drink mint tea, and play dominoes for the rest of my days."

He rambled about what he would do with the fortune a ketab would bring: dowries for his daughters, jewelry for his wife. Disappointed, I turned away.

"Wait," he called. "I have something that may help you in a small way."

He rummaged in a heap of oddments, pulled out a square of silk the size of a handkerchief, and spread it on the counter.

Baksheesh craned his neck over my shoulder. "My Most Fastidious Master does not wish to blow his nose."

"Perhaps not," said Daftan, "but he may wish to see where he is going."

It was not a handkerchief but a map of sorts, more a picture than an ordinary chart. Mountains, rivers, valleys were painted in vivid colors. I could even make out the tiny figures of a caravan. No indication of a Royal Treasury, nor had I expected one.

Shira studied it. "Good enough, Kharr-loh. Better than what you have."

It was, in itself, a beautiful piece of work. I asked Daftan how he had come by it.

"My father, of blessed memory, traded a sack of provisions for it," he said. "I was only a boy then, learning the business. But I well remember the little old fellow who claimed he painted it. He called himself Cheshim."

This took all of us a little aback. Why, I wondered, had Cheshim put so much care and effort into it? What an odd coincidence that we had found it. A lucky accident that we had come to Daftan's shop. Still, it made my skin tingle.

"I thought my father was foolish to strike a bargain like that," Daftan said. "And so he was. It has lain here gathering dust ever since; no demand for such an item."

Daftan offered to throw it in with the rest of our purchases, at so modest a price that Baksheesh did not take the trouble to haggle over it.

I folded it up and stowed it in my jacket. Promising reliable delivery of our supplies, Daftan wished peace upon us and we stepped out into the street.

As we started back to our khan, I felt a hand grip my arm.

26

Hanging on to me, not to be pried off or shaken loose, was a chubby little man, his face round as a full moon, cheeks glistening as if they had been buttered.

He looked so glad to see me, I assumed he was selling something.

"Benevolent fate has led you to my door," he said, smooth as oil mixed with honey. "The stars aligned to light your path. Or did someone recommend me?

"In any case," he went on, "you have found your way to my shop. Welcome, dear friends. I, Khabib, stand ready and eager to provide what you require."

What I required, I told him, was a ketab. I doubted that he had one.

"I have something more valuable," he said. "My clients come from far and wide, seeking the benefit of my excellent services.

"Dreams," he added. "As I am proud to call my establishment the Bazaar of All Dreams."

"Hold on there a minute, Kaboob or whatever you call yourself." Baksheesh cocked an eye at him. "Just because we're strangers in town, don't take us for a flock of gullible pigeons to be plucked. We're not innocent simpletons—not all of us, at any rate. You pretend to sell dreams? What, like some sort of fig vendor? "

"Pretend? " returned Khabib. "Not in the least. Dreams are my stock in trade. Sell? No, I do not sell. I offer the opportunity to buy. And you, my friend—no offense, but you look as if you could use a few."

Baksheesh snorted. "I get my dreams free."

"Of course you do," Khabib said, with kindly concern. "Only tell me this—we speak in all confidentiality—don't you find them, uh, shall we say just a little threadbare? A bit shabby? Worn around the edges, as it were? The same tiresome stuff again and again? And not very durable?

"I daresay," he continued, "they fall to shreds as soon as they've begun. I'll wager they barely last you through the night. Am I correct? "

"Maybe," Baksheesh grudgingly replied. "But that's my business."

"No, dear friend," said Khabib. "My business."

By now, he had nudged and prodded us a short way down

the street. He stopped in front of a narrow-fronted, ramshackle building I hadn't noticed before.

"Come, come." He waved a pudgy hand at the door. "By good fortune—that is to say, your good fortune—I have no appointments at the moment. There are four of you? So much the better. As a special favor, because I like you, I offer a wholesale rate at a most attractive discount."

The notion of a dream bazaar sparked my curiosity. The chubby little fellow was no doubt a faker, a charlatan, full of glittering promises more wind than substance—a combination irresistible to any natural-born chooch.

Baksheesh, however, squinted a suspicious eye on this peculiar merchant. "Assuming you're not a complete liar, how do I know you won't try to palm off shoddy goods?"

"My dear friend, I have a reputation to maintain," replied Khabib. "You shall choose what you please. With every item, satisfaction is guaranteed."

"I, for one, am very interested," Salamon said, making no attempt to hide his eagerness. He was, in fact, bubbling over. "Whether he is a fraud or an honest dealer, the experience will be unique and surely noteworthy."

To please him, we all put aside whatever doubts we had and followed Khabib into his dimly lit shop.

At home, I had often run errands to the pharmacist— Uncle Evariste suffered onslaughts of indigestion and fluxes, no doubt brought on by me. The tall jars, globes of colored liquid, bunches of dried herbs fascinated me. But, until now, never had I seen such an array of bottles, phials, jugs, and flasks of all shapes and sizes. They filled Khabib's shelves and covered the walls from floor to ceiling.

"My inventory." Khabib spread his arms. "Every dream registered and cataloged."

"Mirza Khabib," Salamon put in, "allow me to inquire. How do you conduct your business? You must have clients who come to sell as well as buy. By what method do you obtain your stock?"

Khabib winked and laid a finger on the side of his nose. "Trade secrets. Mysteries of the profession, so to speak. I assure you each item is certified to be in working condition.

"What it comes down to, as do most things in life, is the question of price. Some—I dislike the term *secondhand,* since hands have nothing to do with it—have been intensively used. Those are at the lower end of my range; but all excellent value for the money."

He stepped over to a wall of pigeonholes and waved a hand. "These are the dreams of the dead," he went on. "Acquired before their demise, of course. Highly colorful and entertaining; with surprising endings, as expected from those about to leave us. But, alas, not greatly in demand.

"And these, for a little more, are the dreams of an

insomniac. Poor fellow, he suffered so much from sleeplessness, they have hardly been touched.

"And this—" He suddenly wrinkled his nose and pulled down a phial. "Pooah! What's this nightmare doing here? A small oversight in shelving."

He threw it into a corner. "And now, going to the very top of my line. My special, private reserve, of interest to the most discerning clients of exquisite taste and sensitivities.

"Strictly fresh, pristine condition, never dreamed before. I am proud to say these are available only from myself. If you are hesitant about the expense, I must point out: In my long experience, one gets what one pays for."

"Don't take any of his cheap dreams," Baksheesh whispered to me. "Who knows where they've been?"

I told Khabib we wished the best he could provide. Yet, with so much variety, I had no idea where to begin or what to choose. I asked him to guide us with recommendations.

"It will be my pleasure," he said. "I shall count it an honor of the highest degree if you trust me to pick the product most fitting to your needs."

"I wouldn't trust him to pick my nose," Baksheesh said under his breath. "But since we're this deep into it, let him do whatever he does."

"One small detail." Khabib turned to me. "A delicate matter, a subject I always find embarrassing. A little crass, a little vulgar, especially when dealing with clients of such refinement."

He raised an apologetic hand. "Forgive me, but I must mention it. My firm policy: Cash in advance."

"And my firm policy," replied Baksheesh, while I produced the coins Khabib demanded, "I buy nothing blindfolded. A pig in a poke, as the ferenghis put it. I'll just take a look at what you have in mind to foist off on me."

"The procedure does not permit it." Khabib snapped shut his cash box. "You can't see until you've already seen, so to speak. You understand that, of course."

"What if I don't like it?" returned Baksheesh.

"Hardly possible," Khabib assured him. "Such a thing has never happened. Dear friend, I stand behind my merchandise.

"Ask anyone. They'll all tell you no one is more reliable. However, in the extremely unlikely event that you are not completely satisfied, I shall, of course, replace it. Naturally, there would be a modest fee for extraction, reconditioning, repacking, wear and tear on the product—"

"I knew there was a catch somewhere," Baksheesh retorted. "One other thing. All said and done, bought and paid for, it's mine. I get to keep it. No coming at me later and telling me the lease has run out, or some other sort of chicanery."

"The transaction is permanent," said Khabib. "You own it, exclusively yours in perpetuity. Do as you please, use it whenever it suits you, as often as you like. My merchandise is durable, it won't wear out.

"Or, simply keep it in storage," he added. "Summon it up from time to time; on a special occasion, perhaps. It stays fresh. It will, I assure you, last indefinitely."

"So you say, so you say." Baksheesh shrugged. "Well, it's not my money being flung about. Go ahead, Kaboob. Get on with your business. But I'll be keeping an eye on you."

27

Being fitted for a dream, I supposed, would demand at least as much time and thought as being fitted for a pair of trousers.

Khabib, however, went about his work very briskly. He paced back and forth, sizing up each of us with a quick glance. His lips moved slightly, as if he were reciting the multiplication table in his head.

After only a few moments, he nodded, satisfied by his calculations or whatever they were. Salamon impatiently shifted from one foot to the other. Baksheesh kept a leery eye on Khabib.

Shira—I had never seen her much frightened by anything. But now she looked on edge. Which made me wonder why I let us be tangled up with a so-called dream-seller. Rubbing his hands, flexing his pudgy fingers, Khabib, for all I knew, could be a murderous lunatic at worst; a plump-cheeked swindler at best.

My curiosity got the better of my concerns. He had, so far, shown no interest in trying to murder us; whether he was a swindler remained to be seen.

Khabib ushered us past a beaded curtain and into a dim hallway. I could make out a row of open doors. He motioned for each of us to step through one of them.

I found myself in a stuffy little cubicle. Khabib lit an oil lamp on a wooden table. I had somehow expected us to stay all together. I did not like being separated, certainly not from Shira.

"The procedure is private and personal for each individual," he said when I raised that question. "Have every confidence. I am, after all, a professional."

He pointed at a low divan strewn with cushions. "I shall return momentarily. Be at ease, make yourself comfortable."

As if such a thing were possible in this stifling chamber. It had a heavy odor of stale perfume. I stretched out, neither at ease nor comfortable. To my surprise, and despite my apprehension, I began feeling drowsy.

Khabib soon popped in again. As best I could see beyond my heavy eyelids, he carried a milky glass phial and some other objects on a tray.

With his back to me, I could not guess what he was doing

at the table. The lamplight made his shadow loom enormous on the wall.

He hummed a little tune, like any carpenter or cobbler going about a long-familiar and somewhat boring task. After a time, he came to peer down at me.

"Excellent," he said. "You're doing splendidly."

It seemed to me I was doing nothing at all. Between his being a murderer or a swindler, I began favoring the latter.

He produced a silver cup about the size of a large thimble and told me to drink it down straightaway. When I put it to my lips, I could have sworn it held nothing.

I was starting to get impatient. I asked when his rigmarole would be done.

He blinked at me. "Done? Why, my dear young friend, it has been done already."

In that case, I said, where was my dream?

"Look around you." Khabib made a vague gesture. "Look— but don't open your eyes."

I believe he went away after that. I tried to do as he instructed, and found it more difficult than I expected. For a moment or two, I saw only darkness. Disappointed, I would have gotten up from the divan and gone after him. My arms and legs paid no attention to what I ordered them to do.

Then, suddenly—and I'll say this much for Khabib's merchandise—it was marvelous. Shira was there. But where? Were we in Keshavar? The hills above Magenta? I couldn't be sure. It didn't matter. We were tender and loving, we made discoveries, we laughed. A poem kept drifting through my head. I had never heard it before, but I seemed to know it by heart:

> I gave you flowers;
> You gave me a flight of doves.
> I gave you pomegranates;
> You gave me songs.
> I gave you ripe figs;
> You gave me voyages. . . .

At one moment, we were standing by a riverbank. Shira had woven a wreath of willow branches; so beautiful, but I recalled no more. Khabib was prodding me awake, hauling me to my feet and out of the cubicle. Shira, Salamon, and Baksheesh were in the hallway, all of them glassy-eyed, as I must have been.

Khabib herded us into the shop. Now that he had done his part of the business, he was eager for us to be gone.

"Thank you for your patronage. Recommend me to your friends," he said, hustling us along. "Now, if you please, I have other appointments."

Before I stepped out, he took my arm. Drawing me aside, he cocked his head and gave me a buttery smile. "Did you have a pleasant dream, Messire Carlo Chuchio?"

Later, even after I got my wits about me, I couldn't remember having mentioned my name to him.

So here we all were in the street, rubbing our eyes in the blinding sunlight, with Khabib calling peace upon us and banging his door at our heels.

I stood there, still befuddled, trying to get my bearings. I suppose we were all curious to compare notes and find out what Khabib had sold us; but I had no intention of telling my dream. If Khabib's methods were, as he said, private and personal, the same applied to his product. I meant to keep mine to myself.

Not so with Salamon. He was bubbling over. "Magnificent," he said, completely enraptured. "Remarkable. Most noteworthy, indeed. I had reached the sea. Yes, goodness me, I was on the shore, at the water's edge. And there, shining in front of me, stretching as far as I could see, why, I believe there was no horizon at all.

"Just as astonishing, all my old friends were there. My schoolfellows, too, young as we had been in those days. We laughed, embraced, so glad to see one another."

"And?" said Baksheesh. "What next?"

Salamon blinked at him. "I don't understand—"

"Didn't you splash around? Have a swim? Put at least a toe in the water?"

"No, not at that moment. Khabib woke me up, you see. He

told me there might be some left over for another time. But this was wonderful enough."

"Well, old Sarsaparilla," Baksheesh said, "it doesn't take much to satisfy you."

"Oh, I was more than content," replied Salamon. "I only hope yours was as delightful as mine."

"That lard-faced pickpocket!" Baksheesh snapped. "Oily sneak thief! Slithering serpent in the oasis of my existence! I've a good mind to get my money back—your money, O Noble Master," he added to me. "I'll shake it loose of him—"

I couldn't resist asking what he'd dreamed.

"I went home," he muttered.

"Then," Shira said, "it was a happy dream."

"So what if it was?" Baksheesh retorted. "That's beside the point. It was ridiculous. Impossible. I never had a home."

28

Baksheesh kept grumbling about getting his—or my—money back. Face shining, Salamon was still caught up in his vision of the sea. I would have started on our way to the khan; but Shira, saying nothing until now, held my arm and we lingered a little behind them.

"Kharr-loh," she said, "you did not speak your dream."

"Neither did you," I said.

This did not seem a very good answer. She had her eyes on me, giving me an odd sort of look, waiting for me to go on. And so I had to—no, the truth is, I wanted to.

I intended to be frank and forthcoming, but that turned out more difficult than I thought. For parts of the dream, I found no words that made any kind of sense. Some of it—maybe the best moments—I meant to keep to myself. Though it came out in confused bits and pieces, I did tell her what I could.

When I got to the part about the verses, I had to pause. There were other lines; I couldn't quite bring them to mind again.

Shira had been listening closely. "Yes, there's more."

With that, she repeated word for word exactly what I had dreamed, as if answering me:

> I gave you blood oranges;
> You gave me four seasons.
> I gave you tamarinds;
> You gave me sunrise.
> I gave you a caged bird;
> You set it free.

I stopped short in the middle of the street. It can be off-putting, even a little frightening, to have your own dream recited back to you. There was a reasonable explanation. It was no doubt an old, well-known poem. She must have read or heard it before.

I interrupted to suggest this. Shira shook her head.

"No," she said. "I had the same dream."

I stared like an idiot, trying to make heads or tails of it.

"Khabib!" I burst out. "What's he done?"

He must have made a mistake. How else had he given the same dream to both of us? Or—and this puzzled me still more—had he done it on purpose? Why? Was he a swindler, after all? Had he meant to cheat us?

Baksheesh was motioning for us to hurry along. I had to find out. I turned and ran to the shop. Shira called something to me. I didn't catch what it was.

Khabib's door was locked. I tried to force the latch. It had been bolted from inside. I knocked hard. No answer. I pounded with all my might.

By then, I was in such a state that I considered kicking his door off the hinges. Meantime, a street urchin had sauntered up. He stood, hands on hips, observing my efforts. Even his rags looked impudent.

"They say all ferenghis are mad," he remarked. "I think this must be true. Why, mirza, would you wish to break down a perfectly good door?"

I stopped for a moment. I had already skinned my knuckles, they had begun to smart. I told him, not too politely, it was none of his business, I wanted a few strong words with Khabib.

"Not home," he said. "He is never home."

Now I was out of patience. "I may be a ferenghi, but I'm not a fool. I was there a minute ago. He sold me a dream—"

"Did he, now?" The boy raised an eyebrow. "For a fact? Bought yourself a nice little dream? Where'd you put it? Safe and sound in your pocket? You're a clever one, I see that. Shall you be interested in a sack of fresh air? I'll sell it to you half price."

I had swallowed enough of his sauce. I was tempted to thump him instead of the door.

He went on slowly and carefully, as if I weren't the ripest grape in the bunch. "Mirza, you should stay out of the sun. It will jangle your brain. Let me tell you why Khabib is never home. Because there is no Khabib. There never was a Khabib. So how could he be at home? Also, there is no home. The house is empty, and empty longer than I can remember. But"—he shrugged—"if it amuses you, pound away and peace be with you."

I would gladly have laid hold of him and shaken out a better explanation; but he dodged away and nipped around the corner. Before I could chase him down, Baksheesh hurried up to fetch me.

"O Unbesmirched Innocence!" He sighed and rolled his eyes when I babbled what the urchin had said. "Have you not learned? These Keshavaris will tell a ferenghi whatever pops into their heads.

"Pay it no mind," he urged. "I know exactly what happened. That dream-hawker, that buttery rogue, must have smelt I wasn't pleased with the goods he fobbed off on me. He was afraid I'd want the money back.

"So, nothing simpler. He'll have ducked out a back door. He's lying low, sure we'll never find him.

"Who cares what some ragamuffin street urchin tells you?

Remember, Noblest of Masters, I was there with you. So was old Sarabanda and your girl.

"Now," said Baksheesh, "who are you going to believe? A young layabout having a bit of fun confusing the ferenghi? A natural-born liar who wouldn't know the truth if it bit him on the rear end? Or your devoted, honest, trustworthy servant?"

His explanation satisfied me. It had to. If I thought about it any other way, my wits would have slipped their mooring. What perplexed me: Khabib had addressed me by name. Or had he? I was, at the time, still halfway in my dream; I may have imagined it. Had I told him and forgotten?

I let it go, deciding to trust Baksheesh, always a slender reed to hang on to. But it made me feel better.

We caught up with Shira and Salamon. I said little about what happened, only that Khabib was unavailable, and made no more of it.

At the khan, Salamon and Baksheesh went to tend our animals. We had a lot to do before our provisions arrived the next morning. Especially, I wanted to talk with Shira about the new map.

We sat at a table in the khan. I unfolded the map that Cheshim had painted. Shira seemed distracted, barely studying what roads to follow. She only mentioned vaguely that we were fairly close to her caravanserai.

"Good," I said. "You'll soon be home."

"And then? What am I to do about you?"

I didn't answer. On that question, I assumed, she had already made up her mind: nothing.

She looked away. "Salamon was right, the first day we met him. Do you remember what he told me? There were things I didn't want to know."

She said no more for a while. I waited. She turned back to me, her eyes set on mine. "One thing I didn't want to know, that I was afraid to know: I loved you from the start."

Well. And well. That sent my heart into my throat. Between suddenly dumbstruck and deliriously happy, all I came out with was an eloquent mumble.

"Yes," she said. "I fell in love with you many times. When I saw you on the quay at Sidya, when you were seasick and green as grass. And you still thought I was Khargush the Rabbit.

"And again at the inn, when you were jumping around like a madman in your underdrawers. And again when you thought you were defending me against that pig of a trader. And a dozen times after that. Except when you took my horse.

"I called to you when you ran to Khabib's shop. I understood, then, I had to admit it straight out, not hide from it. Khabib made no mistake. He knew exactly what he was doing. He gave us what we wanted most.

"Kharr-loh," she said, smiling, "who but lovers dream alike?"

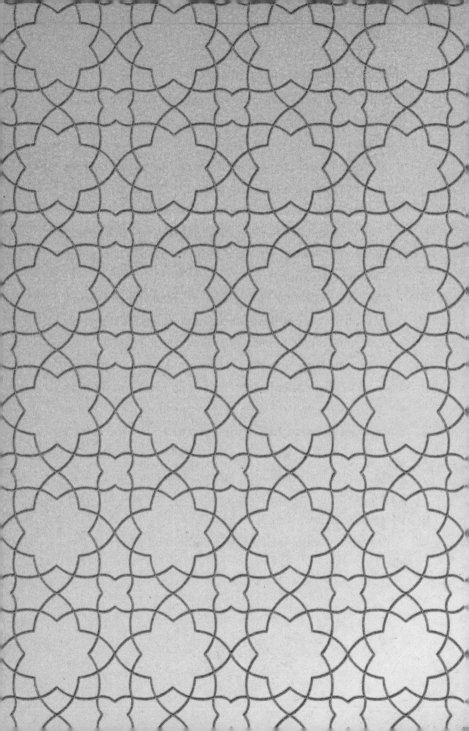

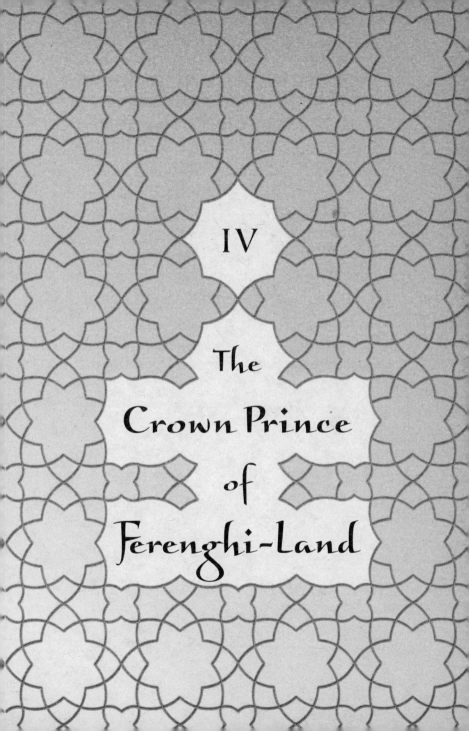

IV

The
Crown Prince
of
Ferenghi-Land

29

I wasn't as happy as I should have been. After what Shira
told me, I imagined we would be closer than ever. Instead,
during the days that followed, she kept mostly to herself,
withdrawn into her thoughts. Something was painfully amiss. I
couldn't quite put my finger on it until I realized she had
never answered her own question: What to do about me?

Nor did I have an answer. It hung constantly chafing in my
mind. I had to force myself to pay attention to the everyday
details, such as not getting lost again. I was still the karwan-
bushi, though in name more than anything else.

Luckily, we met no serious difficulties. Cheshim's map
was accurate—in large terms, if not always in small ones. Sometimes, we found no trail where a trail was shown to be. Then we
would have to backtrack and scout out a different path.

The landscape changed the farther south we rode. The
slopes grew gentler, well watered, green with woodlands; later,

I glimpsed vast stretches of grassy meadows. Still streaked with snow, the highest mountains I had ever seen rose behind us. Since they were not in front of us, I actually enjoyed the sight.

We stayed generally in good spirits, Salamon more eager than usual.

"Marvelous!" he said to me one day. "Our young lady will soon be at the end of her journey." Then he added, "And what of yours?"

I told him I didn't know, it remained to be seen.

"Of course, of course," he said. "What remains to be seen is always the most interesting."

When I asked about his own journey, he smiled happily.

"Mine, I'm glad to say, will have hardly begun. Whatever else, I shall certainly press on to the sea."

As for Baksheesh, he rarely had fewer than three mishaps a day, usually when he was needed to do something useful. Mornings, for example, the camels would gleefully spit on him; afternoons, the donkey might try to kick him; before sundown, he predictably sprained his back when he tried to light our cook fire. Between times, he kept up his ordinary grumbling. But I had the impression his heart wasn't in it, and that he complained mostly for the sake of staying in practice.

By my reckoning, we were now less than a day's travel from the main road and Shira's caravanserai. I counted on reaching it comfortably by the following afternoon. I believe we would have done so if my plan hadn't begun to unravel.

It started when Baksheesh nearly lost a camel. It would seem difficult to lose a camel in open country. Baksheesh came close to succeeding.

Salamon had led the donkey to drink at a nearby streamlet. Shira and I were busy setting out our midday meal. Baksheesh should have been pitching our tents; but I heard him yelling at the top of his voice, calling down every dire threat he could come up with.

One of the camels had slipped its tether and was ambling across the pebbly ground toward the edge of the under-brush. I ran to help Baksheesh, who was flapping his arms and shaking his fists. Out of natural contrariness or deliberate mischief—I swear it had a wicked glint in its eyes—the creature would change course and lurch a handsbreadth from our grasp.

We were both winded by the time we got hold of that humpy, knobby-kneed prankster. Baksheesh began flinging insults at the creature and all its ancestors. He choked on his words. I froze where I stood.

I had been too busy chasing the camel to pay attention to anything else. I hadn't noticed a string of horsemen, six or eight of them, bearing down on us at an easy canter. I learned, later, they had been following along, observing us from the screen of woodland. At the time, they seemed to have sprung out of the ground.

They reined up a little way from us. Big, loose-limbed, in sheepskin vests, they sat their magnificent mounts as if they had drawn their first breath astride a saddle. The horses whickered and tossed their heads; the riders studied us through narrowed eyes long accustomed to looking into great distances.

They showed no inclination to attack. I would have gone to greet them. Baksheesh took my arm.

"Make no sudden moves," he warned. "If you value your Most Esteemed and Precious Life—and especially mine— don't put so much as a finger on that tulwar you've been dragging around." In a low voice, he added, "Mercy be upon us, they're Bashi-Bazouks."

I admitted I'd never heard of them.

"Then, O Blissfully Unaware," he said, "you're the only one in Keshavar who hasn't. Nomads. Wanderers. Here today, somewhere else tomorrow.

"Horse-breeders," he went on. "The best in the country— in the world, most likely."

That seemed a harmless enough occupation. What, I asked, could they want from us?

"Only all we've got," Baksheesh said. "They are a tribe with a very odd way of looking at things. They believe any outsider who sets foot on their lands—and their lands are wherever they happen to be—well, to put it plainly, these Bashi-Bazouks claim the right to whatever the outsider brings with him. It belongs to them. Goods, animals, everything. They have other customs, as well. Best not think of them."

In spite of his warning, I would have drawn my tulwar.

"No, no," Baksheesh pleaded. "They'd dice you up before you could blink. Stand fast. Smile a lot. Look happy. I'll deal with this."

He was off, then, heading toward the riders, making great salaams at every step.

The leading horseman had already dismounted: a black-bearded man who looked as if he had swallowed a barrel, with arms thicker than a pair of Magenta hams. Hoops of gold dangled from his ears; he wore a jewelry shop of gold chains around his neck, and heavy bracelets on his wrists.

I decided to leave my blade in its sheath.

The bearded man stood, arms folded, while Baksheesh made expansive gestures in my direction. Shira and Salamon had, meantime, come beside me.

He nodded, finally, and strode after Baksheesh, who was hurrying to us.

"Bashir, the Horse Master," Baksheesh said in my ear. "The sar, tribal chieftain, and everything else in these parts. Be calm and dignified, Glorious Nobility. I'll speak for you."

Baksheesh stepped aside as the big fellow approached. With all his ornaments, he jingled as he walked. He bowed deeply, then took my hand and pressed it to his massive brow.

"Be gracious," Baksheesh whispered. "Accept his courtesy as if you deserved it.

"I told him you were Chooch Mirza," he added, "Crown Prince of Ferenghi-Land."

30

It wouldn't have surprised me too much if Baksheesh had once again fobbed me off as the dauntless warrior al-Chooch. By no stretch of the imagination, however, had I expected him to come up with a claim so breathtakingly ridiculous.

Bashir's troop had, by now, walked their mounts closer and drifted into a loose circle. For a better look at the Crown Prince of Ferenghi-Land? Or to surround us?

True, Bashir had offered a courteous welcome. He did not draw the enormous, wavy-bladed knife at his belt; nor did his riders point their lances. Still, I was far from comfortable with the royal rank suddenly bestowed on me.

I silently cursed Baksheesh, as I felt threatened more by Bashir's narrow-eyed scrutiny than by any weapon.

"Bashi-Bazouks are folk of honor," he declared, after he finished inspecting us as if we were livestock; and I had done my best not to squirm during the course of it. "To speak truth is law and custom. Lie to Bashir at your peril.

"Now, this one who claims to be your servant, this sway-backed, spavined bag of bones: Winged Mare of Truth has never set foot inside his tent.

"Bashir knows judging of horseflesh. But judging of Crown Prince? Where are jewels? Fine garments? Scarecrows are better dressed."

"My royal master does not wish to call attention to himself," Baksheesh put in. "He travels modestly, to further his education among the commoners."

"Hold tongue when Bashir speaks," our host—or captor—commanded. "What can be seen cannot be concealed.

"Your camels are well tended," he went on, "and handsome donkey. This gladdens heart of Bashir, for outlanders treat their beasts of burden like dumb brutes.

"That much is in your favor, and recommends you more highly than babblings of flyblown servant. But what seals Bashir's judgment is: horse. It strikes eye. Who but prince would possess such a steed?"

Shira looked ready to protest that the mare belonged to her, thought better of it, and kept silent.

"Only Bashi-Bazouks breed horses like that," Bashir declared. "Famous through all Keshavar. Lineage cannot be mistaken. She comes from bloodline of Great Mare. As do we."

"Indeed?" Salamon put in. "Your people believe they are descended from a horse?"

"Yes. Long time back," said Bashir. "Before ancient sires journeyed from Hinda, on other side of mountains. We journey ever since. We call ourselves 'Children of the Wind.'"

"Fascinating," Salamon said. "I must make a note of that."

"You," Bashir said to him, "judging from gray hair—what you have left of it—you are prince's wise counselor and adviser. Is correct?"

"Alas, no," Salamon said. "I have scarcely any wisdom. Advice? I prefer to give none at all."

"There speaks greatest wisdom," replied Bashir. "Anything else is ignorance.

"But you?" Bashir turned to Shira. "Only half ferenghi. The rest, Kirkassi, plain to see. So, then, you are his guide?" Bashir raised an eyebrow. "Perhaps a little more, yes?"

"Horse Master," Shira said, looking squarely at him, "what I am is my own business."

"Well answered!" Bashir clapped his hands. "Filly of spirit, bold as women of Bashi-Bazouk. That is pleasing to Bashir."

Nodding approval, satisfied by his opinion of us, he turned to me again.

"Bashi-Bazouks are free people. Go and come as we choose. Live by our own ancient laws. Crowns? Princes? Their words command us no more than mule breaking wind. Bashir says 'Pfui!' on them all.

"You, Chooch Mirza, you need a little more meat on bones. But heart is good. So Bashir gives you welcome."

I thanked him several times, which seemed the wise thing to do. In a language I had never heard, he called out orders to one of the riders who galloped off into the woodlands.

"Now you come feast with Bashir," he declared. "Sing. Dance. Good times. You stay awhile, grow big and strong."

I thanked him once more and told him we deeply appreciated his generosity, we were honored by it. I added we had pressing business elsewhere.

The Horse Master's bearded chin shot up. He leveled a hard eye on me. "Hospitality offered is not refused. That is law. Or do you fling insult in face of Bashir?"

"What my noble master was about to say," Baksheesh hastily put in, nudging my leg with his knee, "yes, we have urgent business, but he is more than delighted to lay it aside. Behold his impatience. He can hardly wait to feast with you. A privilege, an opportunity not to be missed. He is carried away by joy."

"Is so? Good," said Bashir. "At first he does not look like it. But, with ferenghis, who knows what goes on in their heads?"

Shira, with Baksheesh and Salamon, went to collect our gear and animals. I did my best to appear joyful, hoping it would be joyful enough.

We started off through the woodlands. Bashir walked his horse beside me—either out of companionship or to keep me within arm's reach. He had given his opinion of us. I was glad it had been favorable. As for my private opinion of him, I had the impression he was capable, one moment, of clapping me on the back out of good fellowship; or, the next, punching me in the nose.

I wondered if Baksheesh had overblown the Bashi-Bazouk custom of stripping outsiders of their belongings. It seemed unlikely Bashir would invite us for dinner only to rob us for dessert.

I raised that question, but trod very gingerly around it.

"Not true," Bashir indignantly protested. He shrugged. "Oh, well, from time to time. It depends."

Depends on what? I wondered. The state of his digestion? The weather? The phase of the moon? It did not make me any easier. What he next told me started my blood running cold.

"Two ferenghis come not long ago. Red one with crooked nose. Dark one strutting like king of world. He wants to buy horses. Does Bashir sell?"

Since that was his profession, I said I supposed he did.

"Nah!" Bashir cried. "Why? Because he does not please Bashir. Let him buy horses in bazaar somewhere. He does not deserve horses of Bashi-Bazouks.

"Minds of ferenghis are twisted," he went on. "Bashir not understand them, but knows villain when he sees one. Dark one is up to no good. Bashir has sharp ears, and hears when he talks aside to red one. Of tribute from robber bands in trade for allegiance, for new kinds of weapons, for pots of fire. Who knows what that means? Does he set himself up to be chief of all bandits? Warlord?"

Bashir snorted. "Those like him come and go, try to make themselves master of Road of Golden Dreams. They are fools. No interest to Bashi-Bazouks."

So, I asked, he took nothing from this man?

"Should have. To teach lesson." He shrugged. "Bashir has better things to do. Pfui! Let him go to Jehannum. Play warlord there."

"What if it happens?" I said. "What if one day they come against you? Burn your grasslands, take your herds?"

"Come against Bashi-Bazouks?" He boomed out a laugh. "Chto! Our horses will squash them under their hooves like little bugs."

Bashir looked so pleased and satisfied with himself that I couldn't help being nettled. As Crown Prince of Ferenghi-Land, I decided I was entitled to answer him back.

"That may be so," I said in what I hoped was a princely tone. "Do you care only for yourselves? Let me put it another way. If your neighbor's house caught fire, wouldn't you help put it out? As a matter of honor? Or at least to keep the fire from spreading to your own house?"

"Ha! Wrong!" he burst out. "You know nothing. Bashi-Bazouks have no neighbors. Not live in house. Live in yurta."

What a yurta was, I had no idea. Bashir snapped his jaw shut, delighted he had trapped me in my ignorance. There was something else, but I was afraid to ask. I didn't want to hear the answer. I asked anyway.

"Did this man tell his name?"

"Nah. Who cares? Ferenghi names sound like coughing and spitting. But—yes, red one speaks to him as—what was it? Charkosh."

I knew it in my bones; and with him was the ruffian we had faced on the way to Marakand. I had to talk to Shira and Salamon. They, and Baksheesh, were behind us leading the animals. I would have gone to them, but Bashir draped an arm across my shoulders.

"Forget them, my princely friend," he said, more as a command than a suggestion. "Who cares about gorgios?"

I had not heard that word before. I understood, later, it was not a compliment. It applied to anyone who had the terrible misfortune not to be a Bashi-Bazouk.

We had, by now, come out of the woodlands; and there spread the grasslands I had only glimpsed in passing. They stretched as far as I could see, hemmed by the distant, snow-capped mountains.

The encampment lay just ahead. I had expected a few tents, but it was nearly the size of a small village. The yurtas Bashir had spoken of looked like big beehives wrapped around with blankets of felt; wisps of smoke threaded from holes in the tops. There were spacious pens for livestock; and an open area amid the ring of yurtas—the biggest surely Bashir's, where sat a thronelike stool in the shape of a saddle.

If these folk were wanderers, as Baksheesh claimed, it surprised me they could move so quickly. As we drew closer, I realized the yurtas had been raised around frameworks of slender poles, and the pens were of the lightest wooden laths. The whole camp could be struck, rolled up, loaded on pack animals, and vanish in a twinkling.

Bashir's outrider had spread word of our arrival. All in the encampment must have dropped what they were doing and crowded the open space: the men in sheepskins, bucket-shaped hats of fleece with horsetail trimming; the women, long-boned, in rainbows of swirling skirts, decked out in almost as many bangles and bracelets as the men; youngsters garbed like their elders, dashing about and getting underfoot; and all of them whooping and whistling.

Our escort joined other horsemen lined up by Bashir's yurta. I thought of the Magenta City Troop turned out for a special occasion; except this was a lot more colorful and wilder. It was a grand welcome in honor of visiting royalty; though Bashir took some of the wind out of my princely sails when he admitted his folk seized on any excuse for a feast.

While Bashir flung himself onto his saddle throne, his wife hurried to greet us, with eight or nine young ones peering from behind her skirts.

There was no way I could have a quiet word with Shira. As soon as our animals had been tended to, we sat on piles of blankets on either side of Bashir, myself at his right hand. Some of the smaller girls brought us wooden bowls with carved horseheads for handles. A couple of older ones filled them with a foaming, milky liquid they poured from leather bags.

"Drink, dear friend. Drink!" Bashir cried. "Make you strong like Bashi-Bazouks!"

He downed his bowlful in one gulp. Not to risk offending against custom, I did the same. I found it to be a sweetish-sourish, sharp-edged concoction with a definite aroma of horse. I was glad to be sitting, for my legs felt suddenly packed with pins and needles, my head about to come loose and spin away on its own. All in all, not too bad.

At the same time, we were being stuffed with food, so much of it I feared I might never stand up again.

"And now," Bashir proclaimed, "and now we dance."

My feet felt too big for my boots. I suggested waiting a little while, maybe a good long while. Bashir took me by the collar. Next thing I knew, I had joined a circle of men whirling around in one direction, women in another.

I caught sight of Baksheesh cavorting for all he was worth. Even Salamon was happily kicking up his heels with everyone else. Shira, flushed and bright-eyed, had linked arms with the wreath of women. It occurred to me, in a fogbound sort of way, I had never seen her dance.

After a time, I pleaded for a rest. Bashir had mercy on me. We stumbled back to his yurta. He hunkered down beside me on the ground. I was winded and sweating. Bashir himself looked somewhat woogly.

He rubbed his face with a big hand and knit his brow as he leaned closer.

"Dear friend," he said, "we talk now a little business. You tell Bashir: What shall your ransom be worth?"

31

I had been in peculiar situations, a few more than I ever bargained for. Excepting Shira, I'd have been just as glad to do without them. Now here was the Horse Master of the Bashi-Bazouks, himself big as a horse, who had called me dear friend, earnestly talking about a ransom. As if I were a prize catch.

This would have been bad enough. What made it worse was that everyone else was having a marvelous time.

The dancing had stopped. The revelers, of one accord, began singing, in natural harmony, what must have been their old, familiar songs. Very wild and beautiful they were; merry and melancholy both at once.

And all this going on while Bashir was inquiring what I was worth, as matter-of-fact as reckoning the price a pack mule would fetch.

I decided he was joking.

"You're joking," I said.

"Bashir not joke."

No, I guessed he didn't. The hairs at the back of my neck started rising. Meantime, with night coming on, torches were being lit. Some of the young men had brought out their horses. They galloped around, standing with one foot on their saddles, doing backflips and somersaults while going full tilt, springing to the ground, running a few paces beside their mounts, then leaping astride again. They were amazingly skillful; despite my present circumstances, I couldn't help but marvel at them. The onlookers cheered and whistled through their teeth. Shira, Salamon, and Baksheesh were somewhere in the crowd, happily unaware of my predicament, probably cheering, too.

Was there, I wondered, any way we could simply cut and run? Our animals were—where? Penned among the livestock? Without them, we had no chance. With them, we had no chance. The horsemen would have ridden us down before we got clear of the camp.

Bashir was not as fuddled as he had seemed. He kept a very clear eye on me. So I tried speaking quietly and reasonably, no doubt my first mistake.

"Bashir," I said, "you offered us hospitality. Is this the hospitality of the Bashi-Bazouks?"

"Hospitality accepted must be returned equal measure. Is ancient custom."

I was beginning to think not too highly of ancient custom. It reminded me of Messire Maldonato, our family lawyer.

"You give feast in exchange?" Bashir said. "Nah, that you cannot. So what else?"

"My heartfelt thanks?" I suggested.

"Bashir take that anyway," he said. "From you, money is easiest. Never worry. No extra ransom, no charge for companions. Bashir is openhanded. So, you be same."

"Gladly," I said, "but there's no way I can repay you enough to make up for all the good things you've given us. I have nothing like that amount."

"Of course not. Bashir understands."

I heaved a sigh of relief. I told him I was happy he saw things my way.

Then he added: "You, Crown Prince. Father, King. Rich king, yes? Was ever such thing as poor one? He pays for you."

"I'm sure he would," I said, "but his kingdom is far away. Too far for word ever to reach him."

"Is nothing. Bashir sends best galloper."

My reasonable discussion was only setting us at loggerheads. A picture irresistibly popped into my head. A Bashi-Bazouk horseman, big woolly hat, shaggy vest, jingling baubles and all, charging into Uncle Evariste's counting room, demanding a fortune to regain his son—not even his son, but the family chooch.

"Bashir," I said, with what I hoped was convincing regret, "I'm sorry. It won't do. It will take too long. It could be years—"

"So?" Instead of giving up his impossible scheme, he persisted. "How long? Who cares? No hurry. You live with Bashi-Bazouks. Sing, dance, ride horses. Be happy. Raise family."

"No," I said, firmly and flatly, so there would be no mistaking my determination. "I can't do that. I won't."

"You will." He glowered at me. "Bashir has spoken. No one goes against word of Horse Master. That is custom. That is law."

A dangerous glint came into his eyes. His jaw was set. I knew he wouldn't budge. I had to try another way.

"All right, I'll stay here," I said, while he nodded happily. "But you let the others go."

This was not so much a noble gesture as a practical one. If it came to that, yes, I'd have given my life for Shira. Though, if at all possible, I would have preferred not to. I would rather be alive with her than dead without her. The simple reality: If I stayed behind, I stood a better chance of escaping on my own, and finding her later.

Bashir chewed his beard. He looked slightly less menacing for a moment. But only for a moment.

"Nah, nah. Bashir has no heart to keep you from

companions, least of all from Kirkassi girl. Lovers, not so?" He nodded. "Yes. Bashir sees what he sees. Settled, then. As Bashir wills."

We were at the end of it. I had held back one last thing, reluctant even now to tell him.

"There is no crown—" I began.

"What, you wear hat?"

"No crown. No prince. No ransom. There will never be a ransom," I said. "I'm what you see. Nothing more."

Bashir jolted back. He sucked in a long breath. When he blew it out again, it seemed to come from the soles of his feet, winding up through the rest of him as part groan, part growl.

"Is bad," he finally said. "Very, very bad. Your servant—truth not in him. But had he no better sense than play false with Bashi-Bazouks? Worse, with Bashir himself?"

"For all he knew, you meant to rob us," I hurried to explain. "He was only protecting me. A lie? Yes, but such a small one. In Ferenghi-Land, we do it all the time."

"Not in Ferenghi-Land now." Bashir glared. "With Bashi-Bazouks. You are liar.

"Servant speaks for master," he went on. "Master must answer for what servant does. Servant and master are one. If servant lying, same as you lying. That is ancient code."

I wished he would stop flinging ancient codes at me. "Bashir," I said, "Bashi-Bazouks are horse dealers. Do you mean to tell me you don't bend the truth from time to time?"

"Only with gorgios. And who counts gorgios? Not speaking truth is mortal insult."

"I didn't know. I'm sorry," I said. "But now I've told you the truth."

"Have you?" Bashir laid a shrewd eye on me, and frowned so deeply his face folded in on itself. "Maybe you take Bashir for fool? Maybe you lie now. So not pay ransom. Maybe really Crown Prince after all.

"Makes no difference," he went on. "One way or other, at heart of matter is lie. Big, big offense. One of worst. Against law, against custom, against honor."

I was caught in a cleft stick and couldn't wiggle out of it. "Let us go our way. No hard feelings. All I can do is beg forgiveness."

"Not possible," he said. "Insult so big can only be washed out."

"Then I'll gladly wash it out," I said. "How?"

"With blood," he said. "Yours. Or mine. You offend Bashir, you fight Bashir. To death."

I don't know if I turned pea-green or ash-white.

Bashir had his high spirits back again. He could just as well have been looking forward to another feast. He gave me a good-natured slap on the back that would have shaken my bones if they hadn't been shaking already.

"Tomorrow we fight. Till one of us be dead," he said cheerily. "Tonight, sleep good. Peace be upon you."

32

Bashir ordered a couple of his people to lash up a yurta. He was practically licking his chops; he could hardly wait for whatever he had in mind. I could. Looking forward to disaster can be difficult, especially if you happen to be the object of it. I ducked inside, glad to be away from him.

I slumped down on a pile of blankets. I wondered how to break the news to Shira. To Salamon. To Baksheesh, though I was less than happy with him for putting me—and all of us—in this mess to begin with.

They soon crowded in, laughing and chattering, still excited by the festivities. I would have to do this gently, carefully, a little bit at a time.

"Bashir's going to kill me," I said.

That put a quick end to the small talk. Shira stared at me. She probably supposed I had drunk too much of the Bashi-Bazouks' refreshments.

"It's an ancient custom," I said.

"That's hospitality?" Baksheesh put in.

"Be quiet," Shira told him, realizing I was sober and serious.

"Remarkable. Remarkably bad," Salamon said, after I explained how things had fallen out between Bashir and me. "One thing is clear. Not to belittle your abilities, my boy, but if you fight him, I fear you are bound to lose."

I had, ruefully, come to the same conclusion.

"Therefore," he went on, "you must not face him. In fact, you must be gone from here. If Bashir has no opponent, he has no one to kill."

"I can't get out of it," I said. "I have to fight him. What else?"

Shira put a finger to her lips. She went to peer around the curtain at the entrance of the yurta. She warned us to keep our voices down; one of the horsemen was sitting there. And so we gathered close around the tiny oil lamp.

"You have your knife and your tulwar," she said. "Cut through the far wall. Once out, we scatter. We are not far from my caravanserai. We meet there. You can find your way somehow."

I shook my head. I had thought of something like that, I explained. I didn't see it working. I had, as well, tried to bargain with Bashir to let her—all of them—go free while I stayed behind.

"You would have done that?" she said. "Yes. You would."

"Of course," I said.

She gave me what I believed was a melting glance. "Diváneh," she said.

I took it as a term of endearment.

"It means 'crazy,'" said Baksheesh.

"You have it backward, Kharr-loh," she went on. "You are the one he means to fight. If anyone escapes, you do. He has no quarrel with the rest of us. If anyone stays, we do."

She added something that dazzled me more than any melting glance: "You take my horse."

I turned down that offer straight out. "How do we know he won't come up with another ancient custom to let him do something just as bad to you? I won't let you take the chance."

That put us back to where we started. We sat awhile, not saying much of anything. I did not mention that Charkosh had been there to buy horses. For the immediate future— assuming I had one—it was far down on my list of things to worry about.

More than that, I didn't want to get Shira stirred up again. It had been a good while since she showed any enthusiasm for going after that villain with one of our knives.

Baksheesh had been unusually silent. I had never seen him so downcast.

"Exalted Worthiness," he began, when he finally spoke

up. "I didn't mean for any of this to happen. Can you forgive me?"

Apart from a passing moment when I would have enthusiastically wrung his neck—of course I forgave him. It only surprised me that it troubled him so much.

He perked up a lot after that. "Blessings on you, O Marvel of Mercy," he said. "Do you remember, long ago, I swore to defend you unto death? I gave you my word—"

"It's all right," I said. "I never expected you to keep it."

"Neither did I," he said. "But now I see only one thing. Since I put Your Entirely Admirable Head at risk in these perilous straits, leave it to me. I will pluck you out."

I wasn't so sure about that.

"The only one to fight," he said, "must be: myself."

"Diváneh. Crazy as Kharr-loh," Shira said. But her voice had a fond tone; I knew she was as touched as I was. "If it comes to that, I stand a better chance than you. Bashir will kill you before you have time to scratch yourself."

"Has anybody killed me yet?" Baksheesh said. "A few have tried, none succeeded."

"No," I said. "I won't let you. I can't, even if I wanted to. Bashir won't accept it."

I explained to him that as Bashir was following one of the Bashi-Bazouks' ancient rules, there was no way he would go against it.

"I see a reasonable possibility," said Salamon.

"That's more than I do," said Baksheesh. "Go ahead, Saltimbanco. Let's hear this scheme of yours."

I listened carefully while Salamon explained what he had in mind. I understood his reasoning. It did make sense—of a sort and up to a point. But I wasn't sure it could work.

"Nor am I," he admitted. "But it is not impossible. And if it is not impossible, then, logically, a measure of possibility exists."

"That's your best logic?" Baksheesh muttered. "I could have come up with that myself."

"A small measure of possibility," Shira said. "For Kharr-loh most of all, a great measure of danger."

"But it is something of a plan," Salamon said. "And, therefore, a little better than nothing."

I took some hard moments to think it over. "I'll try it," I said at last. "I'll have to."

I looked from Shira to Baksheesh. They nodded, no happier than I.

I hoped we would sleep. None of us did, not even Baksheesh. We huddled there with little more to say, alternating between tense and glum. By the time dawn trickled through the crown of the yurta, my eyelids had begun shutting down.

They opened fast. In rolled Bashir, delighted to see us awake.

"Come, come, dear friend," he boomed. "Bashi-Bazouks all up and waiting."

I was in no hurry. I suggested starting later in the day.

"Nah, nah." He gave me a cordial jab in the ribs. "Sooner is better. Why spoil afternoon?"

I asked about breakfast, preferably long and leisurely.

He shook his head. "No eating before fighting. Not good. You throw up. If you die, worse than that. Bowels go loose, you disgrace yourself."

He started herding us out of the yurta. I barely had time to snatch my tulwar. At the entrance, Shira held me back.

"Give me your knife, Kharr-loh."

I did. I was being hustled along too much to ask why.

The sun was rising quickly. It did nothing to take away the chill. As Bashir said, the whole camp had gathered in a half circle a short distance away. No one seemed any the worse for the night's festivities. Bashir's black stallion, looking big as an elephant, stamped the ground.

I should have known horses would be involved. But where was Shira's? I saw only a piebald mare, lean, leggy, with a long, narrow head. She rolled her eyes and curled her lips, as if smiling or getting ready to bite me.

"Good mount, high spirits. One of best," Bashir said. "Win, you keep her. Lose, you not care."

When I asked about the rules, he shrugged. "Only one: No rules."

With that, he swung astride. Roaring "Yah! Yah!" at the top of his voice, he galloped into the clear space amid the yurtas.

Baksheesh gave me a leg up. He handed me a slender lance that Bashir had provided. Shira whispered to me, "You understand what to do?"

I hoped so.

33

Bashir had called my horse high-spirited. I would have called her a disgruntled crocodile.

No sooner had I swung astride than she reared and nearly sent me sailing heels over head; then kicked up her hindquarters. At one point, I swear she had all hooves off the ground, for she landed with a jolt that made my teeth clack. I could barely keep hold of my lance with one hand and grab the saddle horn with the other.

I was glad Bashir had declined to serve a meal. My breakfast and I would already have parted company. To make matters worse, Baksheesh gave the mare a good smack on the rear. She plunged forward, galloping full stretch into the clearing hemmed around by eager onlookers.

When Bashir saw me bearing down on him, his face lit up. He gave a couple of joyful whoops and waved me on. He could have been welcoming a long-lost relative. Except for the lance he pointed at me.

My long-legged crocodile of a horse headed straight at him. I flung away my lance and hauled at the reins with both hands. No more than a foot from Bashir, I was able to turn the mare aside; but not before our mounts collided with a jolt that nearly sent Bashir himself out of his saddle.

For a moment, we were flank to flank, practically knee to knee—a good thing, too. At such close quarters, Bashir could not bring his lance into play. With no suggestion from me, the mare slewed around and streaked ahead of Bashir's mount.

He galloped after us. Afraid he might decide to throw his lance at me like a spear, I bent so low in the saddle that half my face pressed flat against the mare's neck. Some lengths behind, Bashir was yelling indignantly for me to turn and confront him and be skewered like any self-respecting warrior.

This was the last thing I intended. The night before, in the yurta, we had agreed that I must, at all cost, stay away and make no attempt to engage him.

And so I tried to keep my distance. Easier said than done. As we circled around, Bashir, in hot pursuit, kept gaining on me.

Pounding over the turf, I had one flash of completely useless regret, and cursed myself for a chooch. Better for Shira and all of us had I stayed Crown Prince of Ferenghi-Land, awaiting the arrival of a nonexistent ransom. We would, at this very instant, be stuffing ourselves with Bashi-Bazouk delicacies instead of my being chased by an irate Horse Master bent on doing me in; and coming ever closer to succeeding.

Well, so much for that part of Salamon's plan. I didn't blame him, he had assured me it would be dangerous. I hadn't expected it to unravel so quickly.

As for the rest—I dared a glance behind me. What looked like an animated bundle of rags came streaking into Bashir's path. Despite all his bunions, lumbago, and everything else ailing him, Baksheesh moved faster than I had ever seen him.

He vaulted up behind the astonished Bashir and grappled him around the waist. Bashir could not shake him loose. The two of them, struggling, tumbled off the stallion's back. Baksheesh nimbly rolled away to avoid being squashed. The Horse Master had fallen heavily as a load of rocks; he sprawled, stunned. I hauled on my reins, and leaped—though it was more of a lurch—off the mare.

The onlookers began shouting furiously, shaking their fists. Some of Bashir's riders started forward to defend their fallen chieftain. Shira ran to pick up my lance and warn them away. Beside her, Salamon called out to the angry crowd, insisting all had been done properly according to their customs.

Despite his assurances, I was afraid they might come rushing at us. His words, at least, were enough to puzzle them; and they held back, muttering among themselves.

Bashir sat up, still dazed, rubbing his head. As soon as he saw me come near Baksheesh, who was warily keeping his distance, he began roaring at me. "Cheat! Treacherous ferenghi! Cowardly gorgio! How dare break rules of combat? Take horse. Face Bashir again. Alone."

He tried to get to his feet, with a view to breaking me in half. To quiet him down, I had to draw my tulwar and set the point under his chin.

He was clear enough in his wits to realize I had him at a fatal disadvantage. I ordered him to stay where he was and listen carefully.

"For one thing," I began, "didn't you tell me there were no rules?"

"But not two against one in combat of honor," he burst out. "Any fool knows that."

"I'm following your own law," I hurried on, as he ground his teeth and glared at me. "There weren't two of us."

"A ferenghi and also crazy?" he flung back. "You tell Bashir: Who is sorry bag of bones with you?"

"My servant. You know that," I said. "You told me only yesterday: What the servant does is like the master doing it himself. Baksheesh followed my orders. I'm responsible. Servant and master are one and the same."

"Is so," said Bashir. "What difference does that make?"

"All the difference," I said. "If servant and master are the same, there weren't two of us. Only one. Me."

Bashir's brow twisted into gnarls and knots. He chewed over my words for a little while. "Is trick somewhere in this. Deep inside. Too deep for Bashir. But there."

I could practically see his thoughts wandering down winding pathways and blind alleys. Finally, still puzzled, he said, "Is as you say."

The piebald mare, meantime, sidled up and nuzzled my neck.

"Yours," Bashir said. "Good horse. Love her, she love you. You win, Chooch Mirza, whoever you are.

"We staked our lives," he added. "Bashir lose."

"Then it's over," I said. "The offense is washed away."

"Not yet," he said. "Strike now. Quick. Make botch and ghost of Bashir comes to haunt you."

He seriously expected to be killed. It staggered me how he could sit there, resigned to his fate, in good spirits, no hard feelings.

"Is good," he said cheerfully. "Great Mare fly down and carry Bashir away."

What he said next staggered me even more.

"Then, you take Bashir's place. You be new Horse Master."

The mare snorted fondly in my ear. I tried to absorb what Bashir so casually told me.

"You be leader of Bashi-Bazouks. Oh, not too long." He waved at the horsemen. "Until one of them challenges you.

Then fight. No servant this time. When you be dead, he be chieftain. Very ancient custom."

Judging from the look of those fellows, they could hardly wait to get in line. I sheathed my tulwar with a gesture grand enough for all to see I meant him no harm.

"Get up, Horse Master," I said. "I already have blood enough on my hands. I didn't seek it, I didn't intend it, but it's there nonetheless. I don't want yours."

Bashir gaped and stared scandalized. "Is ancient custom—"

"Bashir," I said, "what you call ancient custom is just a bad habit. Somebody did something stupid long ago and you've been doing it ever since. It doesn't make anything better. It only gets stupider and stupider."

Bashir shook his head. "Must do. No other way."

"There is," I insisted. "You declare that this ancient custom is gone. Some of the others, too. No longer followed."

"Is true. Lose lot of good men that way," he admitted. "But—can Bashir do this?"

"You're the Horse Master," I said. "Your word is law, isn't it?"

A huge smile shone through his beard. I suspected he wasn't as eager to see the Great Mare as he let on. "Yes! What Bashir says is how it will be. Start new ancient customs."

He got to his feet and stepped a few paces toward the onlookers. Though I understood hardly anything of the language, I was sure he was pronouncing the end of a good many ancient customs. From the outburst of cheers, I gathered some had never been exactly popular.

He strode back to me. "Not yet done," he said. "Blood must still be shed. You, Chooch Mirza, no more Bashir's dear friend."

He drew the knife from his belt.

34

Bashir clamped one rough hand around my wrist and, with the other, brandished his knife.

"No more dear friend!" he cried. "Better than friend. Blood brother."

Before I understood what he had in mind, he gave me a good sharp nick on my outspread palm. As I yelped, he let me loose and did likewise to himself. He squeezed our palms together. Messy, but a great honor. I appreciated it. Though I would have preferred a cordial handshake.

"Now, brother," he declared, "sing, dance, big feast."

The crowd had gone wild, whooping and cheering. For the end of the more unpleasant customs? For Bashir and me becoming blood brothers? For the prospect of yet another feast?

I had to take advantage of our fraternal relationship.

"Cherished kinsman, blood brother," I said. "A little light breakfast would be welcome, but we really must be going."

Bashir's face fell. For a moment, I was afraid he was going to fling an ancient custom at me. He reluctantly nodded. "As brother wishes."

The Bashi-Bazouks laid out a breakfast nearly as big as last night's feast. We ate at long trestle tables set up on the ground where Bashir, less than an hour ago, tried to send me to the Great Mare. Shira, Baksheesh, and I were tactful enough not to congratulate Salamon on how well his scheme had worked out.

When we had all stuffed ourselves, Bashir belched generously and leaned his elbows on the table. "Now, brother, say where you go in such hurry."

Without going into details, I simply answered that we were heading for Shira's caravanserai.

"Where that?"

I took out my map and laid the silken square in front of him, pointing to our destination.

"With this?" Bashir squinted at it. "Pfui! No good. Bashi-Bazouks never need map. Bashir tell you better, faster way."

While he did so, a couple of his folk brought our animals to us. Salamon beamed at seeing the donkey again. As for the camels, Baksheesh was not overjoyed.

Bashir gestured at Shira's mare, while the piebald snuffled and made googly eyes at me.

"You have new horse, brother. Fine saddle, harness, all. And heart set on you." He pulled me closer. In what, for him, was a whisper, which could probably be heard throughout the camp, he said behind his hand: "Be generous, brother. Why not give other to Kirkassi girl? To please her." He nudged me in the ribs, which nearly made me fall off the bench. "That please you, too?"

Shira sensibly kept her mouth shut.

"Why, brother, that's a wonderful idea," I said. "I should have thought of it myself."

After a few more courses of light breakfast, we packed our gear. Bashir loaded us with extra provisions. We said our farewells then, although it took almost as long to leave the camp as the time we had spent in it. Bashir's family and every-one else embraced us in turn; lastly, Bashir himself.

"Brother, Bashi-Bazouks happy for what you do," he said, hugging the breath out of me. "Ancient custom"—he grinned at this—"to wish you 'bahtolo drom.' Follow good road."

We set off then, Shira and I riding side by side. She leaned over and handed me my knife. "Yours, Kharr-loh. I didn't need it."

I slid the blade into my sash. Why, I asked, did she want it in the first place?

She smiled and said, "If Bashir harmed you—it was for him."

Bashir's directions proved better than my map. Leaving the meadowlands, we moved along at a good pace. Now that my attention was no longer fixed on saving my skin, I could tell them about Charkosh trying to buy horses, and Bashir's opinion of him.

Salamon listened carefully to my account. It was the first time I had seen him less than cheerful.

"Bashir understood the situation better than I did," he said. "Quicker, as well. The bits and pieces start coming together. Things that didn't fit, that made little sense—like some of Cheshim's paintings—yes, I see them a little more clearly. If I'm at all correct, I don't like what I see.

"Did I not tell you, my lad, you could think your way through a stone wall if you put your mind to it and took enough time? Now, do you remember when bandits attacked the caravan?"

I nodded. Oh, yes, I most surely did.

"And their weapons? The caravan master had never seen bandits armed like that. Where did they get them? Stolen? Possibly. But I wonder, now, if Charkosh had a hand in it. What if he turned from trading in slaves to trading in weapons? In exchange for what?"

For money, of course, I said. A share in the bandits' plunder.

"Or something more?" Salamon suggested. "Their loyalty? Is he their master, so to speak?" He shrugged. "If so, we must ask ourselves: Is he raising his own army? Does he mean to control as many trade routes as he can? To make himself a powerful warlord? This fits neatly with what Bashir overheard.

"And the flaming globes in one of Cheshim's paintings?" Salamon went on. "The burned-out villages? The thing that came to my mind was Greek Fire. The recipe was long lost. Dare we speculate that Charkosh found it somehow? That, indeed, would be a formidable weapon.

"The biggest question," said Salamon, "assuming any of this is correct, is what's to be done about it?"

"Well, Saxifrage," said Baksheesh, "you're a longheaded old bird with your logic and all, I'll give you that much. But I can answer you easily: Nothing. Because, there's nothing we can do. And besides, it's none of our business. As the ferenghis say, 'We have other fish to fry.'"

"And so?" Salamon said.

"I suggest we set about frying them."

While I wasn't happy to let Charkosh get away with whatever dirty business he was up to, it didn't concern us.

I was wrong.

"Kharr-loh," Shira said, "I'm afraid."

She was. I saw it in her face. With all we had gone through—bandits, warring tribes, howling deserts, and a few others I had gladly forgotten—I had been terrified fairly often. Shira had never so much as flinched. Why now, practically at her doorstep?

I asked what frightened her.

"Going home," she said, in a pale voice. "It was what I

wanted from the beginning. I thought I could face what I found. Now I'm afraid of it."

Privately, I feared the worst. Yet I told her it was very possible, even probable, her mother and brother were still alive, waiting, hoping she would make her way back to them.

I was lying. She knew I was lying.

By afternoon, we reached Talaya: a little market town she had known all her life. Her household, she explained, bought provisions there.

Instead of going straight to her caravanserai, I suggested stopping here first. The tradespeople should know what had happened. It would, I thought, be a way of softening any bad news. In any case, it could do no harm to find out now. At least it might help her decide what best to do.

Because it had been part of her girlhood, I wanted to like the town. I couldn't. It may once have been a pleasant, pretty place. I didn't find it so.

The dusty market square had only a handful of stalls. The few passersby seemed to be looking in every direction except at one another. We did attract some attention when we passed through the gate. Probably because of our fine horses, as well as our being strangers. Among the fruit and vegetable sellers, Shira saw none she recognized.

"This is not as I remember," she said.

"Nothing ever is," Salamon said.

She did stop at a fruit stand she had known. The present owner could only tell her—and grudgingly—that the old woman who had once ran the business had given it up and now lived alone a few streets beyond the square.

We set off to find her. As we crossed the square, two men hurried up.

"You are the great al-Chooch?" said one, with a hasty salaam. "A moment of your precious time. Quickly, for the sake of mercy. A matter of life and death."

Shira and Salamon had gone on ahead. I hesitated, but the two men began drawing me toward a shabby inn. I barely had a chance to tell Baksheesh to hold my horse, keep an eye on the camels, and wait for me.

"Mirza Zuski will bless you," one said, leading me past the empty common room to a chamber at the rear.

And there he was, at a table, sipping a glass of mint tea. I hadn't known his name until now. Zuski—it sounded like trade-lingo for *cockroach*. The redheaded trader we had run up against near Marakand.

He grinned. "A kindly fate brings us together again. I had word you were seen on your way to Talaya. It is my good fortune."

He set down his glass and stepped toward me. "Well, then, O Fearsome Warrior, peace be upon you."

He punched me in the face.

35

"Mirza?"

A thin voice in my ear, and somebody poking at me. Whoever it was, I wished they would stop. I didn't feel like being poked at.

"Mirza? Are you alive?"

"Probably," I said.

I opened the one eye that seemed to be in working condition. Not that it made much difference. I saw mostly darkness. Some shafts of light came from cracks in what I took to be a wall. They made interesting patterns on the ground. When I got used to seeing nothing, I made out a small shape bending over me. I managed to sit up. A big mistake, for my head felt twice its size and about to fall off my neck.

The boy, as I guessed him to be, crouched on his heels, peering at me with great curiosity.

"I heard they locked up a famous warrior," he said. "You don't look like one. Only some kind of ferenghi."

"How do you know?"

He shrugged. "You smell like one."

"So I've been told," I said.

"What are you called, mirza?"

"Carlo. Carlo Chuchio," I said. "Sometimes Kharr-loh. Sometimes al-Chooch. Or Wonder of the World—"

The boy whistled. "All that?"

"Other things, too," I said.

"Whatever they call you," he said, "you are one sick ferenghi. Stay here."

"I expect to," I said. "Where is 'here'?"

"My house."

He vanished. Too bad. He seemed a good-natured boy. I had probably only imagined him. I was still having trouble sorting out my thoughts. Zuski-the-Cockroach had roughed me up a good bit, then his friends had joined in until they lost interest and I lost my senses.

I took inventory. My money belt was gone, of course. And my tulwar and dagger. They had taken my silk map, but overlooked the bookseller's useless treasure chart, still in my shirt. For all the good that did me.

The most important thing missing: Shira. And Salamon and Baksheesh. I didn't panic. They would be searching for me. I was confident they would find me, sooner or later. So I spent a while hating Zuski-the-Cockroach.

The boy was back again. I hadn't imagined him, after all.

"How did you do that?" I asked. "Where did you go?"

"Wherever I am wanting to," he said. "I have my ways."

It was too dim to see clearly, but I was sure he had a grin twice the size of his face. Along with the grin, he carried a pot of water. He let me drink some, then soaked a rag and dabbed at my cuts and bruises. "Why are they bringing you here, mirza?"

"A long story. It doesn't matter now," I said. "Listen, my lad, whatever your name is—"

"Kuchik."

"Well, then, Mirza Kuchik," I said, "what a fine fellow you are. You can do me a good turn. A personal favor. Get me out of this place."

"I would not wish even a ferenghi to be locked up here," he said. "But not now. Wait for night. If they are letting you live so long."

I didn't care for the sound of that. But something had started nibbling at my memory. My wits were still fuzzy, it took me a while to fish it out. Shira had spoken of a little brother Kuchik. There were probably thousands of Kuchiks all over Keshavar. But—in these parts?

"You have a sister?" I said. "Shira?"

He shook his head sadly. "Once, but no more. This is our caravanserai. She is not here now."

Had I felt better, I'd have been more astonished than I was. Of all places to be locked up! I wondered if I heard him right.

"A man named Charkosh took her away," I said.

"Yes. How do you know this, mirza?" His voice faltered. "So it was. The night he killed our father and mother. She is gone a long time. We hear nothing of her. It may be he killed her, too."

"She lives," I said. I could feel his eyes staring at me.

"This is true?" he cried. "Where is she?"

"We were in Talaya together," I said. "After that, I don't know. I was stupid enough to let a pair of ruffians trap me. There was a redheaded cockroach named Zuski—"

"That one?" Kuchik spat. "A bad man. Bad as Charkosh. But stupid. I am sorry, mirza."

"So am I. It was my own fault. She was coming home—"

"No!" he burst out. "She must not. She must never come near this place. Bad things happen since she is gone.

"That night," he hurried on, "I am afraid. I run out and hide in the bushes. I see him carry her off. I follow after them, to fight for her. They go too fast. So far ahead of me I have to turn back. I do not dare go into the house. Some of his men are still there. I fear they will catch me and kill me."

Once he began his account, he was in such a rush to tell all that had happened that he skipped from one thing to the other, half in Kirkassi, half in a patchwork sort of trade-lingo, and I could scarcely follow him.

The boy had, for a good while, lived like a stray cat on the outskirts of the caravanserai. Dashtani, the housekeeper, had been spared. Charkosh wasn't such a fool as to do away with a useful servant; and Dashtani was clever enough to pretend to serve him.

Clearly, she kept the boy from starving during those early days. She set out plates of scraps and leftovers. During the night, Kuchik would creep from the bushes, fill his belly, then dart back into hiding. If any of the ruffians asked why the provisions dwindled, she would throw up her hands and bewail the storerooms infested with rats.

When things calmed down, he grew bold enough to venture inside the caravanserai itself.

"It is a very old house, mirza," he said. "My mother even thought it was built on top of ancient ruins. Long ago, my sister and I played hide-and-seek in little passages behind the walls. Only Dashtani knows I am there. I hear talk, I know what is happening.

"Long after, Charkosh comes back. Zuski is with him, they are in business together. Dashtani tries to make him tell what he does with my sister. Where is she?

"'In Jehannum with all the other she-devils, I hope,' he says. 'That vixen cost me money. She hasn't seen the last of me. She'll cross my path one day or another. When she does, she'll pay me back. With interest. I'll take it out of her blood and bones.'

"This lets us believe she is alive. When Dashtani begs to know more, he is in such a rage he strikes her. He tells her never to speak that cursed name again.

"And so, mirza," he pressed on, "she dare not come here. If she does, he will surely kill her."

"Where is Charkosh now?" I asked.

"Away. Zuski commands in his place. Charkosh makes many journeys. Dashtani says he deals in weapons, and pots of something that burns hotter than fire. She has word he rides here tonight. Men wait for him. They meet to lay plans, mirza. Very big plans."

So Salamon had guessed right. Charkosh was up to devilry of some sort. Whatever his scheme, it made no difference to me. I had to deal with first things first.

The first of first things: Shira. Had she found out where Zuski-the-Cockroach had taken me? If so, would she come looking for me? Would she realize the danger? Or was she cautious enough to keep her distance? Somehow, I doubted that. What would Salamon advise? Too many questions and no answers. I had to head her off.

"Kuchik," I said, "you told me you could let me out."

"Yes, but you shall wait for dark. If you are being seen—"

"I can't wait," I said. "Do it now."

"Not possible, mirza."

"Why?" I said. "You got in here. I'll go out the same way."

"I think not," he said. "You are a too-big ferenghi."

He helped me to my feet and drew me to a corner of the room. When he showed me a narrow gap, I understood what he meant. I would have to be skinnier than a weasel. It was barely wide enough for him to squeeze through.

"When all is quiet, I come unbar the door," he said. "I shall go with you, or you never find your way."

"We don't have time for that," I said. "Do you know which road she and my friends will follow if they come here from Talaya?"

"Yes. There is only one."

"Good," I said. "Go there. Keep watch. Warn them to stay away."

"And you? This is not a good place for you to be."

"Just go," I told him. "After that, we'll see."

He pondered a moment before he agreed that we had no other choice.

"As you say. Peace be upon you, mirza." He started wriggling through the gap.

"Kuchik," I called after him, "I love your sister."

By then, he was gone.

36

The last thing in the world I wanted was to sit like a penned-up sheep waiting to find out what Zuski-the-Cockroach, or Charkosh himself, had in mind. The only certainty: it would not be pleasant.

What little light there was had begun fading. In those dim remaining moments, I took stock of my situation. I had been tossed into what I supposed to be a kind of lumber room, a catchall for oddments too useless to be stored anywhere else, and too useful to be thrown away.

If I could lay hands on any kind of tool, I might be able to chip at the masonry and widen the gap. I groped through the heap of what felt like rags and old rope and unidentifiable junk, finding nothing that would serve.

For lack of anything better to do, I scrabbled and scratched at the brickwork, only succeeding in leaving some portions of my skin there. The floor of beaten earth was too hard to dig, impossible to burrow into. The heavy wooden door, of course, was barred; no telling what was on the other side, but I heaved and flung myself against it anyway.

I was only wasting my strength. Short of the ground opening at my feet and a genie with a lamp popping up to whisk me away or guide me through a secret tunnel, I was well locked in.

I sat down, at last, and leaned my back against the wall, hoping something else might occur to me. It didn't. In the darkness, I couldn't be sure if my eyes were open or shut. It made no difference, in any case.

The dream I had bought from Khabib—he had assured me I could summon it up on any occasion. This seemed a good one; and so I did, glad to be with Shira in some happier place.

I may have drowsed. Again, I couldn't be certain. Sunlight glinted through the cracks. I heard sounds at the door. I jumped to my feet. Kuchik had done his work, Shira was safe, he was coming to lead me to her.

No, of course not. The door banged open. I was taken on either side by the pair of thugs I recognized as the ones who had lured me away with talk of life or death—neglecting to mention it was my own.

They shoved me down a corridor lined with what I supposed were sleeping quarters and into a large eating room set about with tables and benches. At their ease, munching dates or fingering their calmative beads, sat ten or a dozen men in travel garb.

I gave them only a glance, but enough to see they had to be the finest collection of villains ever gathered in one place at the same time.

Oh, they were no light-fingered pickpockets or everyday bazaar ruffians. These were first-rate villains of weight and substance, who gave orders and were used to being obeyed. Changing a few details of their costumes, it could as well have been a meeting of the Magenta Grand Council.

Except they had killers' eyes. Apart from that, they seemed on the best of terms all around. It chilled me to realize they were warlords who had fought one another and knew one another very well.

Zuski-the-Cockroach was there, standing in front of a table. His face was blotchy and he was sweating heavily, choking on his own rage. I grasped the situation straightaway. I had been in it myself, when Uncle Evariste gave me a public dressing-down in front of my fellow clerks. But this must have been worse than any shame or humiliation Uncle Evariste laid on me. Zuski-the-Cockroach looked as if he were having his skin peeled off. I almost felt sorry for him.

What froze my blood was the man sitting behind the table. I had never set eyes on Charkosh until now. But I knew him. Cheshim, the hermit-artist, had rendered a pretty good likeness in the painting he had shown us. But he had not done the man full justice.

Charkosh, in the flesh, was a lot scarier. No mere painter could have caught that air of brutality. If Charkosh ever smiled at you, you'd wish he hadn't.

If I had felt uneasy or disapproving of Shira for wanting to put a knife in him, I took it all back. Now that I saw him, I wanted to do the same.

Charkosh glanced at me with as much curiosity as he would have given to a slab of meat, then went back to bully-ragging Zuski-the-Cockroach.

"So? This is what you brought me? And why, you fool? Because he once offended your tender sensibilities? You knew I wanted that half-breed she-devil. I told you I had word she was traveling with him. You should have taken her before now. Or did you think you'd keep her for yourself? No, you let her slip away. And what do I have? A nothing."

"The half-breed will follow him," Zuski-the-Cockroach flung back. "It was my plan to get them both—"

"Your plan? Are you the one to make plans? You disobeyed my orders. I put you in charge of Talaya. And then what? You swaggered around with your gang of ruffians. Half the folk left, thanks to you. The town brings no profit. I put up with your strutting stupidity as long as you are useful. But not when it costs me money. Are you holding back a little something for your own purse? Do you have other clever schemes?"

As quarrels so often go, his rage overflowed into every-thing else Charkosh could dredge up, far beyond the failure to lay hands on Shira. He ticked off every mistake Zuski-the-Cockroach had made.

"You fly too high for the size of your wings." His voice had turned stone cold, which was worse than when it had been on the boil. "You need to be brought down a little."

Zuski-the-Cockroach had his fill of browbeating; I couldn't blame him. He took a step toward Charkosh.

"Are you the one to do it?" he said between clenched teeth. He pulled a dagger from his belt and pointed it at Charkosh. "Will you try, mirza?"

Charkosh never moved, only gave him a flat-eyed stare and slightly raised an eyebrow.

A couple of his henchmen had sauntered behind Zuski-the-Cockroach. One of them had already unsheathed his blade. In an efficient, businesslike way, he made a quick thrust. Zuski-the-Cockroach stopped short. His jaw dropped, he made gargling noises. The one who stabbed him gave the knife a good twist and wrenched it free. The two men caught him under the arms before he fell.

Charkosh motioned curtly with his head. Zuski-the-Cockroach's eyes were glazing over, his face still had an air of astonishment. The men hauled him away, his heels scraping across the floor. Charkosh chose a few dates from the bowl beside him, chewed them up, and spat out the stones.

Not one of that distinguished company of villains turned so much as a hair. I suspected they had all been in the same situation and had done the same thing. They probably admired and respected Charkosh for acting correctly.

For myself, it left me shaken. I had seen dead men enough to last me a lifetime; but never one murdered in front of me and in such a matter-of-fact way. As far as I was concerned, Zuski-the-Cockroach would not be missed; but I took no joy in that. Not that I was exactly grief-stricken. I had troubles of my own.

After the body had been dragged out and disposed of, they got down to serious business. I was surprised that Charkosh kept me around, since he thought so little of me. I had, for a second, the wild hope he would let me go. Then wild despair, for I realized I made no difference to him one way or the other. He would get around to me whenever he pleased. At the moment, he had other concerns.

Charkosh did most of the talking, with his colleagues occasionally chiming in to comment or question. In its own way, this was not too different from my uncle and Messire Bagatin going over the accounts item by item. It would have been boring had it not been horrifying.

Again, Salamon had it right. What they discussed was nothing less than taking power over the best stretches of the Road of Golden Dreams; and squeezing tribute from the towns along the way. Caravans, as well, would pay for protection against roving gangs of bandits; which was to say, the warlords themselves. There was even talk of tolls for the use of the larger oases.

For their part, the warlords would stop fighting one another and join forces under Charkosh as villain-in-chief. It was a nice arrangement for everyone except those who weren't robbers. I had to give Charkosh credit. He thought in large terms.

For his part of the bargain, in exchange for a share in the profits, he would provide the newest and best quality of arms.

More than the promise of weapons, what caught the warlords' excited attention was a clay pot. Charkosh held it up for all to see. "Among ferenghis," he said, "it is called 'Greek Fire.'"

Murmurs rippled through the company. One of the warlords spoke up. "I have heard old tales of such a fire," he said. "But, Charkosh Agha, it no longer exists—if ever it did."

"It exists," Charkosh said. "Not long ago, I offered a small amount to the Kajiks and Karakits during their recent disagreement. They were kind enough to test it for me. Their chieftains are here with us today. They will assure you of its effectiveness.

"But, yes," he continued, "the formula was lost. And found. It has come into my hands. I obtained it from a journeyer returning from Cathai. The poor fool knew nothing of what he had; he could not read the language. He believed it was a valuable recipe for meat sauce. The price was high, but it was the journeyer who paid. With his life."

The warlords chuckled appreciatively, as if he had come out with an especially clever witticism.

"I destroyed the scroll it was written on. But the formula is safe," he quickly added. "Locked in my memory. No one else shall ever gain possession of it."

He droned on at length, explaining how the substance could be ignited in a vessel of any size, with a wick or long fuse; thrown by hand or launched from a catapult. It would stick like pitch to any surface—stone, wood, or flesh.

Water, he told them, would not quench it, only sand could smother it. At the moment, he had no more than a small amount; but, he assured them, he would soon have the ingredients in quantity, easily stored and shipped as needed, by camelback or horse and wagon.

The warlords listened intently. They were military men and these details were of professional concern to them. Frankly, I lost interest. Escape was my overriding thought, but I saw no way to do it.

When he finished, they nodded approval. Business over, I expected them to leave. But, at every meeting, after all is said, done, and settled, there has to be somebody who muddies the waters by asking an intelligent question.

"Charkosh Agha," said one, "with respect, would it be possible for you to favor us with a demonstration?"

Charkosh pondered a moment. "If you wish, that can be arranged. Ah. Yes. We have with us an excellent subject. I would have disposed of him in any case. But why be wasteful? He can serve the purpose admirably, as you shall see for yourselves."

All eyes turned to me.

37

I've heard it told that a drowning man sees all his past life flash before his eyes. Never having been in that position, I can't say if it's true or not. As for the prospect of being burned to a crisp within the next few moments—in my case, at least, it didn't apply.

I had no time for useless recollections. My concern wasn't with the past but the immediate future. Of which, it would seem, I had very little.

If anything, I was angry. No. Furious. I was certainly not going to go quietly. If Charkosh wanted my life, he would have to work for it. I could only make things as disagreeable and messy as possible.

"Take him into the courtyard," Charkosh ordered the ruffians at my side.

He motioned for his pair of thugs to haul me outside. I had made up my mind to sell my life dearly; but, much as I struggled and flung myself about, it made no difference to them. They had their work to do, and meant to do it with the least effort. They weren't even annoyed at me. One simply punched me in the head; the other kicked my legs from under me and sent me tumbling through the door.

Charkosh, with the clay pot in his hands, followed. The company trailed after him, glad for some entertainment to lighten a night of tiresome business.

I blinked in the morning sunlight. The caravanserai was much like all the others we had stayed in, but the flagstoned courtyard was larger than I had imagined. The usual arcades at ground level, stables at the far side, a well in the middle. The difference: Shira had grown up here. A lovely setting, with mountains, still brushed with snow, towering in the distance. I hoped she would never set foot here again.

His guests gathered around him. There was no sport in killing a sitting bird, so I expected Charkosh would tell his ruffians to turn me loose. I was already casting about to see where I might run, and wondering how long before he decided to end the amusement.

At that moment, one of the guards came hurrying from the gate and spoke hastily in his ear. I could not hear the man's words. Charkosh frowned. He looked as pleased as if uninvited guests were arriving at his party.

"A war band rides here," he said. "Whose people are they?"

No one answered. The company exchanged unhappy glances. "Are they yours, mirza?" he demanded, his eyes on the one who had asked for a demonstration. The warlord shook his head. "Yours, then?" Charkosh turned to the next. "Or yours?"

"They are not my people." The man's chin went up. "No others were part of our agreement."

"Or perhaps, mirza," Charkosh said, eyes narrowing, "you had some reason not to mention—"

"I have told you, Agha." The man bristled. "Do you doubt my word? Do you call me a liar?"

"Only if you are not speaking the truth, mirza," Charkosh said.

I heard the warlord suck in a sharp breath. His colleagues scowled. They were a prickly, touchy lot of killers, especially sensitive when their honor was questioned.

I don't know what came over me. Pressed hard enough, I suppose even a chooch will snatch at anything to save his neck.

"They are his own men!" I blurted out.

All stared at me. As we say in Magenta, I had set the cat among the pigeons. Or, rather, I had set a big, flapping goose amid a pack of wolves. They puzzled over what to make of it.

"He called you here to betray you," I rushed on, as if I earnestly believed what I was saying. "All of you here at the same time. So he can slaughter every one of you—"

"Silence him," commanded Charkosh, his face livid. "Cut out that liar's tongue." He took a step toward me, as if he meant to do that operation himself.

"Let him speak," cried one of the warlords. "He says what you do not wish us to hear."

In fact, I needed to say no more. As far as they were concerned, everything fell into place. They were on familiar ground. It made perfect sense to them. They had probably done the same thing.

"I wondered, Agha," said one, "why you were so willing to sacrifice one of your own men."

"Not one of mine," Charkosh flung back. "I never laid eyes on him before."

"How, then, does he know your secret scheme?" demanded another.

It may take some vigorous twisting of the facts; but, if you're so inclined, I suppose it's always possible to see things in the worst possible light. A dishonest camel-dealer is convinced his customers are out to cheat him. All the more so with professional robbers and murderers. Once they had that bone in their teeth, they weren't going to let go of it.

They pressed closer to Charkosh. My two ruffians lost interest in keeping hold of me and drew nearer to their master.

"It would suit you well," one of the warlords cried out. "Trap us here and kill us all? So you alone are in command—"

He and Charkosh stood glaring at each other. I wondered if this was the moment to put my head down, act as if I weren't there, and quietly walk away. Meantime, some of Charkosh's people came to gather around, blocking my path to the gate.

"Did you take us for fools?" The warrior drew his tulwar.

"I take you for what you are." Charkosh bared his teeth. He held up the pot of Greek Fire, struck a light, and set the wick smoldering.

"Have a care or this will be for you," he spat out. "I never trusted you from the first. Stand away, son of pigs."

For an instant, there was shocked silence. Then I heard other blades come hissing out of their scabbards.

"Treachery!" someone shouted—one of Charkosh's men or a warlord, I couldn't tell. A wave of fury swept over the courtyard. Flames burst from the clay pot as Charkosh raised it above his head. It flashed into my mind—I had seen that same gesture before, in Cheshim's picture in the cave. The blazing globe, the face of Charkosh twisted with rage—

Who struck him first, I couldn't tell. In the instant, all the warlords were upon him, their blades slashing. He flung himself one way and another to escape their attack. He stumbled forward. Still clutched in his hand, the vessel shattered as he fell.

Flames engulfed him. I felt their heat even from where I stood. He had begun screaming, writhing on the flagstones.

The warlords drew away and turned to face Charkosh's people pressing toward them.

If there was ever a time to slip away, it was now. Black smoke drifted over the couryard. The stench of charred flesh caught in my throat and made me gag. I shouldered my way through the oncoming crowd. No one gave me so much as a glance.

Clear of the fighting behind me, I broke into a run. Open, unguarded, the gate lay ahead of me.

I never got that far.

38

The leading riders of the war band galloped into the courtyard, whooping and yelling at the top of their voices. I threw myself to the ground, wrapped my arms around my head, and rolled away to escape the plunging hooves. In those first moments of confusion, I had no idea whose people they were, and didn't much care. My only thought was to lie low, let them pass, then make a dash for the open road. Something was nuzzling at me and snuffling into my ear.

I ventured to look up, and met the adoring gaze of that long-legged, long-headed crocodile: my piebald mare. I swear she was smiling at me. I realized only then that the ones making such a racket were a troop of Bashir's horsemen; and Bashir himself was roaring "Yah! Yah!" while his riders at full stretch circled the courtyard. I glimpsed a flash of white—Shira's steed, with her astride and Kuchik behind, arms around her waist, hanging on for dear life.

I jumped to my feet and clambered onto my piebald, and she was off into the thick of it. I saw nothing of Salamon or Baksheesh. I was just as glad. This was hardly the place for either of them—hardly the place for Shira. Or myself, for that matter.

I had never seen the Bashi-Bazouks in action. And hoped I never would again. I had the quick impression these were the younger hotheads from the camp, spoiling for any kind of fight, and this was the nicest thing that could have happened to them. Instead of lances, some carried stubby little double-curved bows. They looked the size of children's toys. But they were ferocious weapons. Given a choice between the Greek Fire, still blazing away, and Bashi-Bazouk arrows hissing through the air—I believe I'd have taken my chances with the Greek Fire.

Charkosh's gang of ruffians must have felt the same way. Their greatest ambition in life, at that moment, was to flee the courtyard. On top of that, Bashir's riders whistled through their teeth, and yelled enough to terrify the wits out of anyone but a Bashi-Bazouk.

The company of warlords gave a better account of themselves, but not much better. They were seasoned warriors, long experienced, shrewd in combat—which meant they knew when it was time to vacate the premises.

About half of them ran for the stables, hoping to make their escape on horseback. The rest gave up any notion of recovering their steeds, their baggage, or salvaging anything but their own skins. Bad choices either way, for Bashir's riders went after all of them with their deadly little toy bows and arrows. I wanted only to reach Shira. I urged my devoted crocodile into the press of horsemen, but it was like galloping into a riptide. The piebald and I were spun in one direction, then another.

I did catch sight of Salamon leading the donkey, both calmly picking their way through the surrounding lunacy; on Salamon's face was such a look of wide-eyed, innocent astonishment that I half expected him to make a note of the storm swirling around him.

By the time I reined up near Shira, young Kuchik had already hopped off the white mare. I dismounted as he capered over to me.

"I am finding them," he crowed. "Then my sister goes to fetch those big fellows on horseback. Mirza, I do well, no?"

"You did very well," I said. For the first time, I saw he had the same eyes as Shira.

"I was telling my sister you love her." Kuchik grinned enough for several boys his size. "That is good, too?"

"I believe she knows that," I said. "But, yes, also very good."

She was standing looking down at the still-smoldering remains. My first impulse was to put my arms around her—which I did; not so much a loving embrace but to turn her away. She shook her head.

"I was not afraid to face him when he lived," she said. "Why should I be afraid to face him now?"

Salamon had joined us. "Come, child. You have seen. Now let it be. You need do no more. His life saw to his death, as I promised you."

Meantime, a handsome, gray-haired woman of generous proportions hurried from the main building of the inn. Without being told, I knew this was Dashtani. The two of them ran and clung together. Shira let herself be led inside.

I had given up on Baksheesh. I assumed he was at the encampment, fortifying himself with fermented mare's milk.

He came up behind me, with the camels rolling their eyes and wrinkling their noses. He looked at me with sincere awe and admiration.

"O Valorous One," he murmured, waving a hand around the courtyard. "This was your doing?"

"Not exactly," I said. "Not really."

"Ah." He shrugged. "No matter. What is perfection without a tiny flaw? Intrepid Eagle Among the Planets, killing people doesn't seem to be your line of work."

The Bashi-Bazouks had begun the warriors' eternal chore of cleaning up the mess they had made. Apart from being savaged by the late Zuski-the-Cockroach, and threatened with Greek Fire, I had to face a moment of greatest peril to life and limb.

"Brother!"

Before I had time to take a defensive posture, Bashir seized me in an embrace so brotherly that, having rescued me, he could have spoiled it by squashing me flat. Red-faced, sweat-soaked, he pounded me on the back; and left me hardly breath enough to thank him.

"Chto! What thanks when brother needs brother?"

I believed him; but, short of a better pretext, he would have turned out the whole camp to rescue a cat up a tree. He let me loose, finally, and glanced around the courtyard and inn.

"Not so comfortable as yurta," he declared. "But, is good." He wiped his brow on his sleeve. "Hot work makes big thirst, and empty bellies so late in day."

He shifted from one foot to the other, sucked his teeth, and licked his lips, waiting expectantly.

So—what else could I do?—I invited them all to lunch.

39

If, at home in Magenta, I had taken it on my own authority to invite a horde of sweaty, boisterous, ravenous Bashi-Bazouks for refreshments, our housekeeper Silvana would have crowned me with a skillet. Dashtani took it admirably in stride. She sent Kuchik scrambling into the kitchen. Then, hands on hips, she turned her attention to Baksheesh.

"A lazy ne'er-do-well if I've ever seen one." She looked him up and down. "The pots and pans need scrubbing. And so do you. Off with you, Mirza Ragbag. Make yourself useful."

Baksheesh popped his eyes at her. He stood gaping, at a rare loss for words. Then he did what I had never seen him do before. The rascal blushed.

So did Dashtani. If I hadn't been there to observe for myself, I wouldn't have believed it. But I saw it happen. Hearts on tiptoe, they looked on the verge of rushing into each other's arms. In the event, the more she berated him the more his eyes lit up. My besotted camel-puller ducked his head and hoisted his shoulders, in case Dashtani might decide to give him a clip on the ear instead of an embrace, and made for the kitchen.

Shira, I gathered, was still in the old room of her girlhood. I would have gone to her. Dashtani held me back.

"Let her be," she said. "I told her what happened that night. Leave her to herself."

I went to sit at a table with Salamon and Bashir, who took up room enough for several guests. I had been here only a few hours before; it gave me a chill to remember Zuski-the-Cockroach, the warlords, and Charkosh gladly offering to burn me alive. Now my only danger was that Bashir might give me another bear hug. He settled for a fraternal punch on my arm.

"Brother mine," he said, "you come back to camp with Bashir. Bashi-Bazouks all glad to see you again." He cocked a big eye at me. "Some say Great Mare sent you, and you go soon to be with her."

I said that was flattering, but I hoped not.

"And some say," he went on, "no offense to you, brother, but donkey-man is clever fellow, with much wisdom. He had hand in fight with Bashir. Is true?" He turned to Salamon.

"Lavengro," he said—I understood the term meant one of great learning, an unusual compliment coming from Bashir— "you ride with us? No work, only think wise thoughts."

"Ah, well, a most interesting suggestion," Salamon said. "I take it as a marvelous honor. But the wisdom of wise men is highly overrated. You'll manage very well on your own. No, I shall press on to the sea."

Bashir swallowed his disappointment by swallowing every morsel of food that Kuchik brought. He perked up a lot when Shira came at last to join us. I saw her face was pale and drawn. Bashir clapped his hands.

"And this one? Is Kirkassi, but brave as Bashi-Bazouk. You, brother, you stay with her, yes?"

Soon after, when Dashtani had cleaned out her larder to feed Bashir and his riders, we said our farewells. Bashir still urged us to come with him.

"Must break camp now, move on to new pastures. You and Kirkassi change mind, easy to find our trail. Bashir knows horses; knows men, too. You, brother, have restless heart, Bashir sees it. You learn to be good Bashi-Bazouk. For now, bahtolo drom. Brother, follow good road."

"You, too, brother," I said. "Bahtolo drom. And peace be upon you."

Well, turning myself into a Bashi-Bazouk would have been no stranger than some of the things that happened to me. But, as they galloped from the courtyard, I knew in my heart we wouldn't meet again.

"Whatever else," I said to Shira, "you're home."

"Am I?" she said.

We were happy. I suppose we were. Once word spread that this stretch of road was safe and free of bandits, we could expect travelers to stop and lodge at the caravanserai. Over the next couple of days, stablemen and porters came looking for work. Baksheesh, when he and Dashtani could stop making eyes and tear themselves away from each other, set himself in charge of them.

He turned out better at that than camel-pulling. I saw the rascal scandalized at finding a speck of dust. Dashtani had even cajoled him into taking a bath.

Shira and I had our quiet times together. But I couldn't shake off the impression there were shadows in the corners.

And yet another leavetaking.

Early that morning, Salamon came to find us at breakfast. He had, as usual, passed the night in the stables with our animals.

"I shall miss all of you," he said. "But I've lingered too long. I must be on my way."

It didn't surprise me. I knew, sooner or later, we would part company. I had only hoped he might have waited a little while. What surprised me was Baksheesh, who looked more downcast than any of us.

"Well, you silly old coot," he said, making every effort to grumble and not succeeding at it, "you saved my life. I never thanked you. I thank you now. Dear friend—I'm sorry to see you go."

"Your tender heart has finally got the better of you." Salamon smiled as he glanced at Dashtani. "I knew it would."

"So what if it has?" Baksheesh retorted. "I hate it when people say 'I told you so.'"

"And you, my dear girl," Salamon added, embracing Shira, "I'm glad for you. You've come to the end of your journey.

"As for you, lad," he said to me, "I hope you find what you're seeking."

I took Shira's hand. "I already have."

"If that's true, it would be most astonishing. Count yourself lucky," he said. "But promise me one thing. Take good care of your donkey. He's a fine fellow."

"I won't be able to do that," I said, "because he's going with you."

"Oh? Well, well, my boy, that's very kind of you. We've grown quite fond of each other. Thank you."

We went to the gate with him. He turned once and waved at us while the donkey frisked beside him. Then they were out of sight.

"If he ever gets to the sea," said Baksheesh, "the old codger's likely to start swimming across. I wouldn't put it past him."

Travelers heading west from Cathai began arriving sooner than expected. Unprepared, we all had to pitch in to look after them. I offered to do what I could. Shira gave me a hasty kiss; but, in the business of running an inn, she made it clear I was more ornamental than useful. And so, at loose ends, I was left to my own devices.

Not for long. Kuchik adopted me as his personal property. Whenever he could escape the watchful eye of Baksheesh, he traipsed after me. He was delighted with himself at having saved my life—as indeed he had—and the lives of us all.

He got the notion into his head that I was a dauntless adventurer from the wild and perilous land of the ferenghis. He kept at me to tell him tales of the amazing things I had done.

"Kuchik," I said, "you'll hear more and better from any journeyers who stop here. I can only tell you one thing: Don't believe a word of them."

He shrugged that aside. "Chooch Mirza," he said, "I am wishing to see these things for myself."

"You'll make your own journey," I told him. "When you're ready."

This didn't satisfy him. He wolfed down my account of all that had happened to me. I even tossed in a few things that hadn't. He only licked his lips and demanded more. He was gleeful to know his sister once disguised herself as a boy named Rabbit. He laughed himself into hiccups when I told him how Baksheesh left me frantic in my underdrawers.

By then, I had scraped the bottom of the barrel. At a loss, I finally rummaged through my bag. I found the old volume of tales the bookseller had given me—what, a lifetime ago? Like myself, it was a little the worse for wear, but Kuchik seized upon it. Since the stories weren't in any language he knew, I had to read aloud, translating as I went along. But he was quick-witted, and it took no time until he could read them for himself.

"Chooch Mirza," he said, wide-eyed, "are these wonders being true?"

I had to admit I had never seen a flying carpet or a genie with a magic lamp, or any of the other marvels.

"Are you saying, Chooch Mirza, these are lies?"

"Yes," I said, "but some lies are better than others."

With no duties to occupy me, after our guests were long gone to their beds, I sat up late in the eating room, doing nothing in particular. I had given Kuchik the book, which he greedily carried off; even now, he was probably hiding away somewhere, devouring the print from the pages.

And so it was that Baksheesh found me there at the loosest of ends. Instead of being the first to eat and sleep, he was now the last, staying up to make sure all was in order.

Dashtani's bewitchment had been more miraculous than any flying carpet. Though every bit the attentive, diligent innkeeper, there was still a permanent rascal lurking under the clean clothes; and I knew him well enough to see, when he sidled up to me, he wanted something.

"O Generous Heart of the Universe, Bestower of Precious Gifts," he began, which convinced me all the more he had some scheme in mind, "have you turned the Dazzling Sunlight of Your Contemplation on the treasure?"

This brought me up short. I almost said, "What treasure?" So much had happened, I had practically forgotten.

"Noble Master," he went on, shuffling his feet, "do you still mean to search for it?"

I told him I didn't know. I wasn't sure what I meant to do. "Why do you ask?"

"There was a time when you released me from my vow to stay with you—"

"Yes," I said, "and you wouldn't accept it."

"The Clarity of Your Brilliant Recollection gladdens the Heart of the World, O Noble One. So now I ask if your generous offer still applies?

"In the dream that faker Khabib laid on me, I went home—though I never had one in the first place. Home? It was this caravanserai I dreamed of. And someone waiting for me—"

I told him he needn't spell it out. Wherever I went, he was free to stay at the inn.

"A thousand blessings on you!" the rascal burst out. "A million—"

"One is more than enough," I said. "Go and tell Dashtani."

He sped off, faster than I had ever seen him move. I sat there. I hadn't thought of the old map until Baksheesh and his blathering brought it to mind. For the sake of old times, I pulled it out and spread it on the table.

I hadn't looked at it—for how long? Poor map, it had seen better days. I had found it in the binding of my book of tales. Uncle Evariste, I well remembered, had crumpled it up and thrown it at my head. I had salvaged it as best I could. At least, it was all in one piece; but there were deep creases I had never been able to smooth out.

It still baffled me why anyone would go to the trouble of drawing a map that was wrong; above all, one that supposedly showed a hidden fortune. As Shira had pointed out, some parts of it were accurate; the rest, no use whatever.

I started to fold it up again. The map fell naturally into its original creases. And others I hadn't noticed. It looked as if someone had pleated it at random. One corner had been dog-eared, turned down to overlap an edge of the parchment. There were, on the back of the sheet, what I had taken for meaningless scribbles. When I folded the page over, the lines and squiggles turned out to be indications of roads, rivers, and mountains that fit exactly with the pleated page.

Folded thus, it gave a whole different picture of Keshavar. The map had not been drawn carelessly.

It had been drawn to deceive.

If it had fallen into other hands or been seen by other eyes, it would have appeared to be only a badly sketched, faulty diagram. It wasn't.

It was perfect.

I could trace every road we had followed. Where the words "Royal Treasury" had been lettered, the map ended. At Shira's caravanserai.

The fortune was here, beneath my feet.

40

How often does the family chooch find himself sitting on top of a fortune? I stared at the map. It stared back at me. I knew, down to the marrow of my bones, it had shown me its secret.

In the same way I had folded the parchment, I fitted together the bits and pieces of what I had learned without realizing I was learning anything at all. They matched. The more I thought of it, the clearer the picture grew. Kuchik had offhandedly mentioned the inn had been built over ancient ruins. Shira herself had told me the legend, handed down from her mother: The Dark Fortress. How Tarik Beg had betrayed his own people, let them be slaughtered at his gates, and buried their wealth under the floor of his treasury.

Admittedly, yes, I dreamed of finding a treasure trove. I never seriously dreamed of what I would do with it. At another time—long ago, as it felt—another place, in other circumstances, I'd have figured that out fairly quickly. Dazzle Uncle Evariste and all Magenta. Spend it. Waste it. Likely get bilked out of it. Or, imitating Zameen, the well-digger in the old tale, acquire palaces, herds of camels and horses, and chests of jewels to impress his beloved Aziza.

Not in this case. For one thing, I hoped I knew better. For another, it wasn't mine to dispose of.

Ordinarily, I would have sprung up and roused all the household to announce my astonishing discovery. Instead, for what remained of the night, I sat there quietly, wondering how to tell them. Wondering, even, if I should tell them at all. Would it be wiser to say nothing?

Sitting on a fortune? I was also sitting on a disaster.

At first light, the several travelers who had passed the night packed their gear and rode their camels from the inn. I called Shira and Kuchik, Baksheesh and Dashtani, to gather around.

I explained about the map, showed them how I had found its secret; before any of them could break into cries of amazement, I hurried on.

Assuming, I told them, the map was exact—as I believed it was—Tarik Beg's royal treasury lay buried deep beneath the caravanserai. But precisely where? Below the main buildings of the inn? The stables? Under the flagstones of the court-yard? How big an area? How far did it reach? And here was the disaster:

To unearth the treasure, we would have to destroy the caravanserai.

Kuchik's eyes got brighter the longer I went on. "Then, Chooch Mirza," he piped up, "we must begin our digging right away."

"That," I said, "is for your sister to decide."

"We share all of this," Shira broke in. "The place is his as much as mine. Let him speak his thoughts."

"With all these riches—" Kuchik was hopping up and down; I expected him to jump out of his skin at any moment. "We need no caravanserai. We shall be buying camel trains. Horses. Elephants! I can be starting on my journey—"

"Kuchik," I said, "elephants, flying zebras, or anything else, it will be a long time before you journey anywhere. Your sister will have something to say about that."

Dashtani, listening silently, had gone pale. She turned her eyes to Shira. "Child," she murmured, "my whole life has been here. Would you tear it down?"

"You have been a second mother to Kuchik and me," Shira said. "You have an equal voice in what we do."

I didn't hear anyone asking for Baksheesh's opinion. He offered it anyway.

"What, no consideration for my feelings? My dream promised me a home. And a sweetheart. That's worth more than a mountain of diamonds! And you mean to take it all away and break my heart? No, I won't stand for it."

"Baksheesh, I honor your tender feelings," I told him. "It's still for Shira to say."

"Kharr-loh, do you truly wish me to speak my mind?" she answered. "Then so I shall. The home I came back to is not the home I left. There are too many memories of too much grief.

"Tear down every stick and stone," she said. "It will ease my heart."

"If that's your wish," I said, "the matter is settled."

"No," she said. "I speak only for myself. I give the others' wishes the same weight as my own. But we are evenly divided. Kuchik and I on one hand. Dashtani and Baksheesh on the other.

"You are the one who sought a fortune. You are the one to decide."

I said nothing at first. Inside my head, I could hear Salamon's words when he learned I was seeking treasure. What a shame if you should find it, he had said to me. Your quest would be over. And then what? No, the journey is the treasure. I had not understood him at the time.

"The fortune belongs to the dead," I told her. "Let them keep it."

"As you choose, Kharr-loh," she said.

Shira was gone; no sign of her upstairs or down. She must have left soon after we all had talked together. I went to the stables. At sight of me, my doting piebald whinnied and tossed her head. Shira's horse wasn't there. The stable boy could only tell me she had ridden from the caravanserai.

I saddled my piebald. We cantered across the courtyard and through the gate. I had never been there, but I had seen the spot before: in Cheshim's painting.

Near the riverside, her white mare browsed amid a stand of willows. Shira knelt at the water's edge. She was weaving a slender branch into a circlet.

I climbed off my horse and went to her. "I knew I'd find you."

"You always do." She held up the circlet. "When journey-ers cross the river, they carry wreaths of willow. So they'll remember where they came from.

"I've talked with Kuchik," she added. "He's happy to stay with Dashtani and Baksheesh. I wouldn't have gone without telling you."

"Gone where?" I asked.

"To the place I dreamed of long ago." She stood and motioned toward the farther shore. "For the sake of the child I was. I love my home, I always will. But I love it as it used to be. I can't stay here. *I gave you a caged bird; / You set it free.*"

"*I gave you ripe figs; / You gave me voyages,*" I said. "I can't go back to Magenta. I've been away too long and come too far. Weave a circlet for me. I'm going with you."

She smiled. "I thought you might."

I asked what we were looking for.

"Whatever we find. Salamon and his donkey may reach it before us, but we'll press on to the sea. Kharr-loh, I won't leave you again."

"You never did." I held out my arms. She came to me. "I already dreamed this."

"I know," she said. "I was there."